One Bite

Stories for
Short Attention Spans,
Stolen Moments,
and Busy Lives

John Sheirer

Propaganda Press
Publishing Branch of Alternating Current
Palo Alto

Acknowledgments: Most of these stories, sometimes in different forms, have been published in the following print, online, and audio publications: *43 Things; 50 to 1; 52/250; 100 Word Stories; 100 Word Stories Podcast; 101 Words; Acme Shorts; Adventures in Adulthood; Amphibi.us; Apollo's Lyre; Blink-Ink; Booksie; Boomer Times; Boston Literary Magazine; Buzzle; Camel Saloon; Cautionary Tale* (and the anthology *The Best of Cautionary Tale 2008); Christian Science Monitor; Cuento; The Cynic Online Magazine; Down in the Dirt; Drifter's Oasis; Espresso Stories; Flashes in the Dark; Flash Party; Flashshot; Ficlets; Fictional Musings; Fiction Press; Fifteen Minutes of Fiction; Five-Word Monologues; Foliate Oak; A Handful of Stones; Helium; Humor Press; Idling; In Between Altered States; Ink, Sweat, and Tears; The Ladies Room; Laughter Loaf; The Legendary; Litsnack; Litvision; The Logos; Love Blender; MuDJoB; My Very Worst Date; The New Flesh; The Northville Review; Obsidian River; One Million Stories Creative Writing Project; One-Screen Stories; One Sentence; Paragraph Planet; Personal-Political; Pittsburgh Flash Fiction Gazette; Postcard Shorts; Pow Fast Flash Fiction; Raw Nervz; Redbubble Flash Fiction; Scrine; Seedpod; Seven by Twenty; Ship of Fools; Short Humour; Short, Fast, and Deadly; Six Sentences; Six-Word Stories; Softcopy Three-Line Story Contest Winners; Storyhouse; StoryJoin; Storymania; Synchronicity of Indeterminacy; Talk to Action; Two-Sentence Stories; Weirdyear; Word Catalyst; Word Riot; Word Slaw; Writing.com's Amazing 55-Word Story Contest Winners.*

Book design: John Sheirer and leah angstman
Editor: leah angstman
Title text: Handwriting–Dakota
Body text: Garamond

ISBN 978-0-578-08264-6

Propaganda Press
PO Box 183
Palo Alto, CA 94302, USA
alt-current.com
alt.current@gmail.com

for Daisy
the best dog in the world
1994-2011

Just Beyond the Deer-Crossing Sign

Deer crossing.

Argument

Even her stomach growls at him.

Clueless

Hummer vanity plate: AVG JOE

Middle of Nowhere

A huge sign reads, "Free Parking."

Suicide Discussion

She offers to pay for the next lunch.

Fascist Statement?

"No," she said. "*Fashion* statement."

Four-Way Stop Sign

All four drivers wave each other through.

Overheard at the Salad Bar

"Never," she said, "not even with my husband."

High School Reunion

The guy they all called "kid" has the most gray hair.

Theology

Writing about his soul, he enters the "save" command.

First Date

How charming, that fragment of broccoli caught in her teeth all evening.

Unemployed

He measures progress in phone calls, letters written, and flowers watered.

Late

An hour late for dinner, his wife calls to tell him she hasn't met another man.

Kindness

"Kindness," he said, and she laughed like he was the silliest little boy in the world.

It's a Long Story

Thinking of his wife, he accidentally said, "I love you" to his boss's answering machine.

Karma

At the new-age bookstore, the clerk just smiled as the shoplifter ran out the door.

The Most

"He loved me the most," whispered ex-wives from all four corners of the funeral parlor.

Seven Years Later

For about half an hour after he awoke this morning, he couldn't remember his ex-wife's name.

Better Looking People

After making love, Gwen and Andy watched better looking people make love on late-night pay-per-view cable.

Friday Afternoon

The note had been on his office door for more than three hours on Friday afternoon: "Back in five minutes."

Bitter

"My ex-wife called me petty and bitter," he said to his lawyer. "Don't be silly," his lawyer replied. "You're not petty."

Flashback

Feeling like he did as a teenager buying condoms, Sam placed the "just for men" hair dye on the convenience store counter.

Hard Time

The baseball game at the prison came to an untimely end when the lead-off hitter slammed the first pitch over the fence.

Someplace Better

One seat left at the movie, but she scanned the crowd for a full minute—searching for someplace better to sit than beside him.

Update

Ashley's social networking credibility suffered when she tried to use her status update to call Jennifer an *idiot* but spelled it *ideote*.

A Visit From the Irony Fairy

Melanie was surprised to hear everyone complaining about the quality of refreshments served at the world-hunger-awareness meeting.

Middle-Aged Man's First Text Message

Hi Sweetie. I'm in the bathroom at work. I forgot to bring a book to read. But I have my phone, so I'm texting. See you tonight. Love, John.

Seven More

When he told the lovely stranger how much he admired her tongue piercing, she replied, "I've got seven more. How many do you want to see?"

Insomnia

Martha was sure the ab-machine being advertised on late-night TV could change her life—if only the telephone weren't so far away from the couch.

Coping

While waiting in his therapist's office, he wrote another draft of his most recent letter to his ex-girlfriend on the back of a pamphlet about depression.

Third Date

It hit him halfway through dinner—when she told him how much he reminded her of her favorite brother—that the evening would end with a handshake.

Bad News from the Doctor

But that was yesterday, so long ago. Today, the dog sleeps at his feet, sunshine warms his neck, and the neighbor children are playing and laughing just across the street.

Patience

While taking down the Christmas lights, Roger paused to wipe a forearm across his face. "Damn," he muttered, steadying the ladder, "this is one hot July we're having this year."

First Visit to the Big City

From his bus window, Eric noticed a man in a business suit having a heated discussion with a trashcan. From Eric's perspective, the man appeared to be losing the argument.

Thank You for Calling

"Thank you for calling the suicide prevention hotline. We're sorry, but no one is available to take your call. Please leave a message at the tone, and we'll get back to you as soon as possible ... *Beep*."

Critic

While visiting the restroom between classes, the English professor found very little among the stall graffiti to hold his attention, considering half the body parts and sex acts were spelled incorrectly.

Woman Wearing Sunglasses

There she is—indifferent, saying hello, politeness alone. Her gaze is invisible. She's probably not looking at you. And there you are—two inches tall, a miniature reflection of a small man in place of her eyes.

Cheat

As Caroline cheated at solitaire, pulling the king of hearts from her hiding place within the deck, she asked her husband, Ron, immersed in the *World Series of Poker* on television, "Do you ever think about other women?"

Flaws

During their latest argument, she counted off his worst flaws—all eight of them—lifting a finger or thumb for each one. She probably could have named ten flaws, but she was using two fingers to hold her cigarette.

First Time

"You should know," he told her, turning off the lights, "that I have a few scars."

"You should know," she replied, lighting a candle, "that I do, too. But mine are mostly on the inside."

Double-Shift

Smitty was scheduled to work a double-shift that day—fifteen straight hours—so he chugged three bottles of Five-Hour Energy drink. Did it work? No one knows yet because the bureau of missing persons is still looking for him.

Finish Line

While running his first marathon at age fifty, Jake finally spotted the finish line ahead. But why was the finish line bathed in a tunnel of heavenly light? And was that Jake's grandmother floating there, waving and calling him to her?

Forecast

This is how I see it, Alicia thought as she watched the weather forecast alone while sipping hot chocolate on another frigid Friday night. *These TV weather people are a lot like insecure men. They talk and talk about eight-to-ten inches, but it usually turns out to be more like three-to-four.*

Mystery Story

One guy was dead. The other guy held a gun, which was actually smoking when the police broke down the locked door. The guy with the gun was mumbling something about a woman they both loved. It really didn't seem like much of a mystery. But, hey, you never know.

May I Take Your Order?

Monday afternoon, with only twenty minutes to get to another meeting downtown, he waited in line for a drive-thru cheeseburger. As the family in the van in front of him ordered enough food to feed a small country, he realized this would be the only peaceful moment he'd have all week.

Waiting

Ever since he gave the pretty woman at the grocery store his number, he has started bringing the phone with him to the bathroom whenever he takes a shower. But the only time it rings, it's a bill collector named Mr. Lynch, and Mr. Lynch wants to make arrangements for payment while the shampoo burns his eyes.

Elevator

It wasn't until the third visit to her mother's new "active-senior" apartment building that Karen finally realized what had been bothering her about the elevator. It wasn't the tinny music or the stale scent or the ugly paisley wallpaper.

No, it was the fact that the doors were exactly the width of an ambulance gurney.

After Ten Years

"You're insane," he said, his last words to her before turning to leave, his last words after ten years of marriage. "You're like that crazy artist guy who cut off his ear—what's his name, van Gogh? The only difference is that you've been slicing away my life a tiny wound at a time each day for the last decade instead of just hacking it off all at once."

Thank-You Note

We had a wonderful time at your dinner party. It was so kind of you to invite us. Your friends were delightful, and the conversation sparkled. The food was delicious, your home so beautiful. Thank you for taking the time to walk us to our car. Our only regret is that the evening had to end when we saw the stray dog get run over by that speeding truck.

Zen Life Interrupted

Way back when he was sixteen, he tried to meditate. But he couldn't stop thinking about this certain girl he liked. She had red hair and sat in front of him in English class. She knew twenty-seven poems by heart and kept a secret journal written in purple ink and smelled like bubble gum. Anyway, it hurt his back to sit that way, trying to meditate, so he stopped. He just stopped.

Fortieth Birthday

He checked the label again: "Loose Fit Jeans."

That's what he thought it said. The jeans were a fortieth birthday present from his wife, who had just sent him to the bedroom to try them on.

I sure as hell wouldn't call these things "Loose Fit Jeans," he fumed to himself as he sucked in his gut and struggled with the zipper and button.

A True Story About a Place he Used to Live

It was another summer Sunday afternoon, no breeze, just sweltering air. An old man shuffled along the cracked sidewalk ahead of him and talking to himself.

As he passed, the old man said, "Right buddy? There ain't nothin' in Athens, Ohio, is there?"

"Nope," he said, wiping sweat and walking faster, "never was."

Reflection

While she went off to find a new set of bed sheets, he lingered in the bath section. He studied himself in the first mirror, but it was only 3X power. All he saw was the need for a shave. The second was stronger, 5X, but that only revealed a few freckles he didn't know were there. The last mirror was the most powerful. But even in its 10X reflection, he was satisfied that she wouldn't find what he was searching for on his face: guilt for what had caused them to need new bed sheets in the first place.

Vocation

On Interstate Route 81, a few miles south of Scranton, Pennsylvania, there's a large green road sign that reads, "Ashley Sugarnotch." If you take the highway exit one direction, you end up in Ashley, Pennsylvania. If you take the other direction, you go to Sugarnotch, Pennsylvania.

It's sort of comforting to know that if someone had gender reassignment surgery and then tried to break into the adult entertainment industry, he or she wouldn't have to worry about what stage-name to use.

To-Don't List

1) Get up early on Saturday.
2) Let the telemarketer keep me on the line.
3) Buy the same shirt I already have.
4) Keep ignoring that bad smell in the kitchen.
5) Forget her birthday.
6) Assume the ringing in my ears is nothing to worry about.
7) Notice the weather only when it's bad.
8) Depend on caffeine.
9) Allow that jerk to talk to me that way.
10) Make stupid lists.

Lunch Hour

He jumped from the bed where his boss's wife lay giggling. Their lunchtime tryst had lasted longer than expected, and he was late for another meeting where that same boss would certainly notice his absence. His clothes were scattered from the bedroom to the front door, where she had ordered him to strip an hour before. He found and managed to put on his briefs, pants, shirt, tie, jacket, socks, and left shoe—but the right shoe had vanished. They searched until a growl from the kitchen led them to discover $100 worth of Italian leather half-eaten beneath her dog's big paws.

Upstairs Neighbors

All day—Bob's only day off work this week—as he tried to read a new book or watch an afternoon movie or talk with his brother on the telephone, his upstairs neighbors argued. This was their usual argument. "Why were you talking to that woman?" "Hey, you were talking to that man, so I can talk to that woman." The same weary characters and tired marriage plot played out a dozen times before on a dozen other days off gone wrong.

That night, as Bob tried to sleep, just like a dozen times before, all he could hear was their bedsprings squeaking.

Accident Report

Two unidentified hikers suffered only minor injuries after the male attempted to mount the female last weekend in a secluded area of Mount Washington. It seems her bare buttocks and his bare feet simultaneously encountered mossy patches on a rock outcropping during the near consummation of the couple's relationship. The pair slid five hundred feet down a steep incline before coming to rest in a patch of wild blackberries. Rangers reported that the couple plans to return to the spot next month and advised them to wear the proper clothing and footgear needed for attaining their summit.

Job Interview Blues

Stanley should have gotten the job. His references were solid, his experience varied and appropriate, and his education prestigious. He had researched the company, knew its product line and profile in the industry. His résumé sported uniform margins and crisp type. He held eye-contact with every firm handshake. His suit was wrinkle free, and his tie, selected with the help of his saintly wife, Barbara, brought out the blue of his eyes. Under other circumstances, Stanley probably would have gotten the job—if only his Tourettes hadn't made him tell the Human Resources Director ninety-seven times in just under an hour to go to hell.

Chance Meeting

They met by chance at the laundromat. She was a graduate student in human services at the university, preparing for a career in social work. She just wanted to help people. She really was that kind of person.

He ran the fryer at the local fast-food joint, a promotion from cleaning up spilled kid's meals and mopping the slimy restrooms. He told her he was a physician's assistant who volunteered as a Big Brother and served turkey at the city homeless shelter on holidays.

By the time she suggested exchanging phone numbers, he was already thinking about exchanging bodily fluids.

Forgetful

It was like she wanted to show him how much she cared for him and how much she wanted to be with him, so she decided to send him a lock of her hair.

But after she cut that single lock, she decided that wasn't enough to show him how much she really cared for him and how much she really wanted to be with him, so she decided to cut off all her hair and send it to him because that would really show him how very much she cared for him and how extremely much she wanted to be with him.

But then she decided that she couldn't let him see her with no hair, so she ran away for a year to let her hair grow back, and in that time, she forgot about him.

Before and After

Luke stood in shirtless profile before the full-length bathroom mirror, his belly bulging, pecs sagging, shoulders dipped, head slumped, mouth turned down, eyes vacant.

"Before," he mumbled to the empty room.

Then he sucked in his gut, puffed and flexed his chest, pulled his shoulders up and back, jutted his jaw, smiled with his whole face.

"After," he called out.

He reverted to the "before" pose, then arched back to "after" … before, after, before, after, before, after.

Wow, Luke thought, heart hammering, panting from the effort, *I need to figure out a way to get paid for this!*

The Jogger

Every morning around 10, he would jog a few hundred feet and then pull a comb from the waistband of his gym shorts and run it through his hair. That was his routine, every morning: jog a little, comb a lot, jog a little more, comb a lot more. He went around the block maybe three or four times, taking more and more time with his hair and less and less time jogging, sort of giving himself extended cool-down periods. He even jogged on weekends, sometimes getting funny looks from the folks mowing their lawns or raking leaves. He even jogged in the winter, wearing the same gym shorts and running shoes as he mucked his way through the unshoveled sidewalks.

He wasn't in very good shape, but, *damn*, that guy's hair looked *fantastic*.

Somewhere Down There

Somewhere down there in his memory, his high school long since torn down and hauled away to fill a landfill, buried beneath the rubble of countless other demolitions among the gray hard jagged chunks of locker room concrete blocks, among the crushed red brick walls whose sight he cursed each morning from the school bus, among the shattered hallway tiles he shuffled over on yet another trip to the principal's office, within the mangled gym lockers used by his basketball team so bad their own fans booed them, inside his very own senior year locker is his pair of "lucky" socks worn the last game of the year, somewhere down there, through the rubble, through the decades, through the memories—those lucky socks still stink.

Post-Op

It was only minor surgery, after all—snip a little cartilage and drain some fluid. An hour after it was over, hearing his name called, he slipped in and out of awareness. His throat burned from the breathing tube they'd removed. He longed for ice chips fed by his loving wife, the laughter of his children, a nuzzle from the family dog. The pain throbbed but was less than what he'd been told to expect. The bed sheets scratched his face, and he felt heavy against the mattress. As the hours passed, he grew gradually lighter, more aware, and finally lifted himself from the bed. By evening, he wanted to go home.

A week later, after his funeral, he felt fully himself again, ready to haunt those he had left behind, starting with the doctors and nurses who had let him die.

Tuition

Dave knew he had failed the final exam that morning, and he hadn't even started the twenty-page research paper due that afternoon. He needed some inspiration, some encouragement, some motivation. His roommate would be no help, considering he was in the same spot, on the brink of flunking out. His professors would be annoyed that he waited this long to get help. His parents would just say, "I told you so." His girlfriend would dump him if she knew how bad his grades were this semester. If only he could find just the slightest reason to buckle down, get his head together, and salvage some dignity—if not a couple of passing grades. Wishing for words of wisdom, instead he saw this message etched into the wall of his college dorm's restroom stall just above an arrow pointing to the toilet paper: "Your college diploma. Deposit $100,000 and take one."

Sarah's Mother

After dinner, everyone went to the back yard. Summer would end soon, so they wanted to take advantage of the warm evenings while they still could. The kids played on the swing set or chased lightning bugs while the adults at the picnic table drank beer and wine coolers.

Eventually, as the cold descended from the star-filled sky, the fathers grew weary of pretending interest in sports talk and complaining about their jobs, the kids got tired and weepy, and the mothers began dropping hints about going home. Off in the far corner of the yard, Sarah, the only teenager in the group, halfway between a child and an adult, leaned back silently with her mother, each in her own rusted lawn chair.

Just before the first family left, Sarah asked her mother the question she'd been holding deep inside her all evening: "What did the doctor say?"

One hand cupping her breast, Sarah's mother whispered, *"cancer."*

Maybe

Jeff got drunk after she told him, "Really, it's not you—it's me," when he knew *it was him*. Not just drunk, but so whiskey drunk he could barely remember taking the pills, but the bottle was half empty now, so he must have taken them. Not half full—definitely half empty.

He woke at three in the afternoon, tasting dirt, and spent three minutes on the phone with the suicide hotline he found in the phone book.

"Dude," the counselor said, "maybe it really *wasn't* you." Probably a college kid volunteering to pad his résumé, so Jeff hung up.

He considered flushing the rest of the pills. After knee surgery three years ago, they gave him a full bottle of Percocet. *What the hell is with that?* he thought. *Are they trying to create addicts to drum up more business?* Jeff had dry swallowed two pills after the surgery and then forgot he had them until last night.

But he decided not to flush them today. His knee had been hurting a little lately, a dull but persistent ache. He might need the pills again after all.

Happy Holidays

When she was twelve, April's father was transporting the Easter ham from the outdoor grill to the kitchen and dropped it onto the breezeway's concrete floor. April's mother, of course, was furious. Moments later, both parents screamed at each other over the ruined meat. Pineapple glaze, April's favorite, oozed into the pores of that rough floor, built so many years ago by the original owner of their ancient farmhouse.

From that day forward, nothing was the same. Her parents' holiday arguments grew more common as the years passed, making fancy meals an endangered species in April's home. Thanksgiving turkey drumsticks were wielded as weapons. The Christmas roast was lobbed like a grenade and left on the floor as luxurious dog food. Jellied cranberry sauce dripped from walls like Technicolor blood at the multiplex.

Now, so many years later, April has a family of her own. But she's more careful. Her family battles are fought over ordinary plates of fish sticks or peanut butter sandwiches or mac and cheese. Her children will grow up with happy holidays.

Old Trick

Duchess was nineteen—impossibly ancient for a big dog—when Dave brought her to the vet for the last time after a month of lethargy and a week when she didn't eat and rarely left her bed by the fireplace.

For nearly two decades, Duchess had barked at countless delivery trucks, slept in pools of sunshine on hardwood floors for what must add up to entire years, saw three kids off to preschool and eventually to college, ate and pooped a mountain range of kibble, dug enough dirt to bury a city, chased whole universes of squirrels that she never caught.

The vet said, "A good life, a big life." His voice was so kind. This vet had become one of the family's oldest friends. "Maybe it's time for her to rest now."

Dave nodded, ignored the strangle hold on his throat, stretched out a hand for one last touch goodbye.

For the first time in weeks, Dave saw her nose twitch and search, saw a familiar look in Duchess's cloudy eyes as she slowly raised her head a last time.

Just seconds from the end of her life, she was checking to see if Dave's hand concealed a treat.

Jerk

"You're the biggest jerk in the world!"

The woman shouted at Tom as she walked toward him along the sidewalk. He stopped and stared, his mouth agape. *What did I do?* Tom thought. He searched her face for clues, but he didn't even recognize her. How could he have forgotten someone with so much resentment toward him? She stared beyond his shoulder, too angry even to make eye-contact with him.

Tom thought he should say something, but what? He didn't know whether to run and hide or to yell back at her.

Just then a man brushed by him and pushed a rose toward the woman.

"Happy birthday!" the man sang out and wrapped his arms around her.

She pushed him away and glared.

"I thought you forgot, you big jerk," she said, but then laughter broke across her features, and she pulled him into an enthusiastic embrace.

As Tom passed and studied her smiling face, he realized that maybe she did look a little familiar after all.

Curt Had a Great Deal of Anger

Curt had a great deal of anger.

For the third time this month, he had been called into the boss's office and reamed out because his job performance was in the toilet. *Who gives a crap about the way I answer my phone?* Curt thought as he stomped back to his cubicle.

Last week the complaint had been about the way he filled out an obscure form that no one would ever read anyway. *Those forms could be put to better use wiping my ass.* The week before, it had been for spending too much time away from his desk. *I get my work done, so I'm not gonna sit around this dump any more than I have to.*

Curt decided to get even with his boss. *I know what I'll do,* he thought as his face flushed and he shoved open the door to the office restroom, the one on the north hallway that the boss used most often. *I'll eat nothing but high-fiber cereal every morning and take a big crap in here every day, twice a day if I can, even three times, and I won't flush, never. Just let it all there for that big jerk to find. That'll show him. He can't mess with me.*

Yes, Curt certainly had a great deal of anger. But, unfortunately, Curt didn't have a great deal of imagination.

Miss Me?

"Admit it," she said as they left their final court appearance. "You'll miss me."

"Well," he said, "do you remember that time five years ago when I cut my foot on that broken beer bottle? The doctor closed the cut with staples instead of stitches. It took fifteen staples. They stayed in my foot for a month. I kept snagging my socks on them and they'd seep little pools of blood into the sheets at night. They itched all the time, but I couldn't scratch them because I was afraid I'd open the cut. A couple of them got kind of rusty looking, and I thought I might be getting blood poisoning. It hurt like hell when the doctor finally took them out with those weird little pliers. And he almost broke one off because it had actually started to grow into the bone. Then they oozed puss for a couple of days, and I had to go back to make sure they weren't infected. Do you remember all that?"

"Yeah, I remember," she said.

"I'll miss you like I missed those staples when they came out."

She considered this for a moment, and then she smiled.

"I knew it," she said. "I knew you'd miss me."

Ten Lies His Fifth-Grade Teacher
Tried to Make Him Believe

1) On a typical day, every person on earth passes within twenty feet of a murderer.

2) Human beings are made up of three cents' worth of minerals.

3) The average fast food hamburger contains 1.7 inches of human hair.

4) While sleeping, human beings swallow or inhale an average of eight spiders over the course of a lifetime.

5) Every 1.9 seconds, a child somewhere urinates in a public pool.

6) Every 3.8 seconds, an adult somewhere urinates in a public pool.

7) The average bottle of ketchup contains 1.3 worms per cubic inch.

8) Turkeys are far more intelligent than chickens.

9) The Russians established a colony on Mars in 1963, then abandoned it due to lack of funding in 1967.

10) Too much television causes eyeball cancer.

11) (Bonus for extra credit) He would never amount to anything.

Hats for Everyone

Lately his mind had been consumed by thoughts of hats.

What marvelous things hats are! he thought.

He wanted to invent a new kind of hat—the perfect hat—one that could be surgically attached to the wearer's head.

First the hair, scalp, and skullcap would be removed. In their place, the hat itself—made of very strong, malleable, waterproof, dust-repellent, heat resistant, transparent plastic—would be attached. This hat would fit in such a way that it could never be removed. This hat would fit so snugly that it would take on the shapes, colors, and textures of the wearer's brain.

Every time the wearer would have an original idea, a pleasant memory, or a sexual experience, the hat would wrinkle and move and glow in a strange and very beautiful way so that everyone nearby could watch the wearer's hat and share the joy of the experience.

Everyone would be happy for each other—wives and husbands, children and parents, friends and enemies. Wars would end.

How wonderful these hats would be! he thought, and what a beautiful thought it was, a thought we all could share, if only he knew how to invent his new hat.

Janet's Debut

When she was sixteen, Janet sat in the bleachers at Fenway Park watching the Red Sox beat the Yankees seven to six in extra innings. With two outs in the bottom of the seventh, a 3-2 count on the batter, runners on second and third, Janet casually reached under her tank top and adjusted her still-growing breasts to make them more comfortable inside her bra.

The batter struck out, ending the scoring threat.

The television camera caught her adjustment.

Her family back home was taping the game in case Janet made an appearance.

Now Janet is forty-seven, a law school graduate, married for twenty-three years to a cardiac surgeon, mother of two college honor students, and recently appointed a state appeals court judge.

But when her family got together for Thanksgiving dinner this year, and Janet asked one of her brothers—the one who barely finished his first year of college, hasn't held a job for more than eighteen months at a time, and has been divorced three times—"Could you please pass the gravy?" he responded with an announcement that brought peals of laughter from every corner of the table: "Hey, remember that time Janet played with her boobs on TV?"

How One Thing Leads to Another

The day had warmed from the chilly morning to the temperate afternoon, so he paid his lunch check, left his coat on the back of his chair, left the diner, and stepped into the sunshine of the parking lot.

If he had remembered to put on his coat, he wouldn't have noticed a fragment of lint on the front of his shirt. If he hadn't noticed the lint, he would have seen the low air pressure in his front driver's side tire. If he had noticed the low air pressure, he would also have noticed the sluggish handling of his car as he negotiated the entrance ramp to the highway on the way home. If he had noticed the sluggish handling, he would have been more prepared to deal with the downed branch that blocked part of the entrance ramp merging onto the interstate. If he had been more prepared to deal with the branch, he might not have overcorrected his steering and let his passenger-side front tire slip off the pavement onto the gravel. If he hadn't let his passenger-side front tire slip onto the gravel, he wouldn't have flipped his car over the embankment where it rolled seven times before coming to rest in the backyard of a cute little ranch-style house. If he hadn't flipped into the backyard, his future wife wouldn't have run to make sure he was okay.

If he hadn't met his future wife, who would have gotten him the new coat for Christmas that year?

Good Price

Sandra had seen the woman on this street corner before, but she had generally avoided contact as she hurried to work. But this frigid morning was different. The woman wore at least five warm-up jackets, all of them children's sizes but gamely stretching to cover her grown-up body. The woman had layers of T-shirts on under the jackets, along with a wool skirt over ragged men's sweatpants. Still, Sandra could see the woman was shivering.

The woman caught Sandra's eye and spoke. "Could you loan me some money to buy a glass of milk?" Each word floated in a stream of frozen breath between the two women.

"I'm Sandra," Sandra said, watching her own breath stream merge with the woman's words before they dissolved. "What's your name?"

"Hannah." The woman's name hovered in a single word cloud, an island refusing to blow away.

"What's the going rate for a glass of milk, Hannah," Sandra said, reaching into her purse.

"It runs about a dollar in today's economy," Hannah replied.

Sandra knew the money wouldn't go for milk, but she didn't care. It was too cold to care this morning.

Sandra pulled out two worn dollar bills. "That's a good price. Buy two glasses and drink one for me."

Words to Warm a Teacher's Heart

1) Do we get extra credit for showing up to class?

2) I did a few of the assignments and went to class a couple of times. Why did I get an F?

3) I'm done learning for today—can I go home now?

4) I thought you were kidding about that exam thing.

5) Syllabus? Oh, that … I lost that thing six weeks ago.

6) You're not my father! Get off my back! My paper is only a month late!

7) Textbook? You mean we have to buy a textbook?

8) I've missed the last ten weeks of class—what do I have to do to pass?

9) I'm no good at this subject, I have no time to study outside class, and I'll probably be absent half the time—but I have to get an A!

10) My name is Fred, and my speech is about why it's dangerous to wear seatbelts.

11) You gave me a B+. Why do you hate me?

12) How much will I get when I sell the textbook back?

13) Do I have to wait until the end of the semester to sell the textbook back?

14) I saw it on the Internet, so it must be true.

15) Library? I didn't know we had a library.

16) I wasn't in class last time—did we do anything important?

17) So am I going to, you know, like, pass this class, and stuff?

Obit

He often bit his mother's nipple because he liked the taste of blood. He held his baby sister's head under the bath water long enough to know it was wrong. He peed in the corner of his second-grade coatroom instead of walking the extra steps to the bathroom and only stopped so he wouldn't get caught. He broke a friend's finger with a well-aimed dodgeball throw and was happier about the skill of the throw than worried about his friend's finger. He blew his nose on the basketball towels he knew his teammates used to wipe their faces. He told the girl whose virginity he took that she was too ugly to take to the prom. He fantasized about killing the professor who gave him his only failing college grade but just slashed the guy's tires instead. He listed on his résumé three jobs, two awards, and a reference that didn't exist. He borrowed from petty cash four times but only returned the money once. He slept with a coworker two weeks after his wedding. He lied to charity solicitors that he gave to other projects. He started gossip about himself so that he could claim not to dignify it with a response. He got his last promotion with a promise to lay off as many people as possible. He went to Tea Party rallies and waved a flag and cheated on his taxes. He responded to his diagnosis at age 43 by thinking about his new car before his children. He told his wife that his deathbed-wish was that his funeral music feature the Billy Joel classic, "Only the Good Die Young."

Mr. Boots

The last thing Bruce wanted to do while driving through upstate New York was stop at the highway rest area—but he had to. He brought in a book, locked the door, and sat down.

After a moment, someone came in and sat in the next stall. The new neighbor was wearing huge work boots that must have been about size sixteen, so Bruce named him, "Mr. Boots." After a moment, Mr. Boots began whispering very softly. Bruce couldn't tell if he were whispering to him or to himself or to someone else. Bruce couldn't make out any of the words. He wasn't even sure they actually were words.

Then Bruce heard a strange crinkling sound, followed by repeated crunching and more crinkling. He was confused for about half a minute, but then it hit him. Mr. Boots was eating chips while sitting on a public toilet.

Without warning, a chip fell to the floor and skittered a couple inches into Bruce's stall. It was one of those curlicue corn chips that Bruce really liked, salty and satisfying.

They both sat in silence for a long ten seconds.

Finally, Mr. Boots asked, "Are you going to eat that?" in a clear, intelligent, almost refined voice.

"No thank you," Bruce replied.

"Okay," Mr. Boots said, and he reached down to pluck the chip from the floor with a large, clean, well-manicured hand. The hand and the chip disappeared from Bruce's view, moving upward.

A fraction of a second later, Bruce heard the crunch.

Ant Traps

The first day in their new house, the young couple unpacked and kept marveling—such a big place at a reasonable price on a quiet street.

The second day, they noticed the ants. Some were large, meaty things that seemed angered by the invasion of their home. Others were tiny, barely visible, and seemed unconcerned with the humans' arrival, probably because they outnumbered them several billion to two.

The third day, they sought help at the hardware store.

"We need some ant traps," the wife said to the middle-aged man behind the counter. His smile faded, and he looked at her as if she had just threatened his dog.

"You can't get that here," the man said.

"You don't carry ant traps?" the husband asked.

The man seemed offended. "Of course not. I don't even think that's legal."

The husband began a response, sucked air into his lungs the way he did before swear words were about to surface, but his wife touched his arm.

"Well," she said, "We have ants in our new house. Do you know where we can get ant traps?"

The man stared at her for a long moment, and then he spat laughter.

"What the hell is so funny?" the husband asked.

"You want *ant traps*," the man said between chuckles. "I thought you were asking for *anthrax.*"

By the tenth day, when the ants had actually carried away all of the ant traps, the young couple began to wonder if maybe anthrax would have worked better after all.

Blind Date

Ben's coworker Julie had set him up on sort of a male-bonding blind date with Ron, her boyfriend.

"You'd really like him," Julie said. "He plays basketball too."

So Ben called Ron and invited him to the Wednesday night game he'd been playing in for a couple of years. Ben picked him up at Ron's house and drove them to the gym. The conversation was short and not terribly interesting.

"You play often?"

"Maybe twice a week."

"Me too."

"Unless I'm busy at work."

"Same here."

The rest of the ride was silent—not a great beginning.

Warming up, Ron looked like about an average player, nothing special. But the first time down the court, Ron hit Ben right in the hands with a no-look pass for a lay-up. It was perfect. Ben had no idea he was going to throw him the ball, and then suddenly it was in his hands for a fraction of a second just before he put it off the backboard and through the hoop. Then on defense, Ben's man faked him out and was driving to the basket when Ron left his man and fouled Ben's before he could take his shot. Not a great defensive play, but more than enough to keep Ben from looking bad. Later, when Ben hit a game-winning jumper, Ron was the first one there to high-five him. The whole evening went like that. It was as if Ben and Ron had been playing together for decades.

The next day when Ben saw Julie at work, all he could think about was how lucky she was. Ben was sure that Ron was really good to her in bed.

No

Yes, the orthopedic surgeon looks kind of young, Gary thought as he lay on the operating table, settling in for the procedure that would repair his torn anterior cruciate ligament and eventually allow him to rejoin his friends for their Tuesday-evening "old guy" basketball games at the health club.

Yes, I'm old enough to be his father, Gary thought, but the kid did graduate from medical school, and he must have observed dozens of ACL reconstructions, and then assisted in dozens more with experienced surgeons.

The nurse had laughed when she gave him the pen and asked him to write "NO" in big letters on his left knee, the one that had always been strong and healthy, had always managed to compensate for the weak and balky right one, to make sure that the surgeon operated on the right knee, the correct one.

I'll be okay, Gary thought, just as the anesthesiologist said, "Count backward from 100," and Gary barely made it to 97 before the ceiling lights began to swirl and darkness closed around him.

When Gary awoke in the recovery room, he was surprised to see several doctors, nurses, and people in business suits so formal that they could be arguing before the Supreme Court gathered around his bed, each with a very concerned expression, so he asked, just before the pain pounded into his knee through the fading affects of the anesthesia, "What happened?"

"From certain angles," the young orthopedic surgeon said, stepping out from the hiding place behind his elders and barely managing to look Gary in the eye, "the word 'NO' looks a lot like the word 'ON.'"

Dimming the Lights

They met at one of those restaurants with strange knickknacks on the walls: movie posters, sleds, antique kitchen implements. If the place had a theme, he had no idea what it might be. This was a late lunch or early dinner blind date, depending on your daily schedule perspective. He called it lunch—she called it dinner, a bad omen for anyone on the lookout for omens.

His married friends set them up, but she was all wrong for him—so were his friends, when he allowed himself to think that way. He was looking for a fun date, a few laughs, maybe something more to lift his spirits. But the whole thing had simply turned generically dull, the way blind dates do when one person realizes after ten minutes that things are not going well.

The big problem was that she had a pessimistic comment for everything he said. "I like biking," was met with, "My brother broke his hip in a bike accident." "These glazed pecans really add sweetness to the salad," prompted, "Yeah, fat and calories too." But he trooped on through most of the meal, holding up both ends of the conversation as best he could between her downer comments. After a while, he just stopped saying much of anything.

When the restaurant lights dimmed at five (the official transition between lunch and dinner), he squinted at the dessert menu, ever optimistic.

"I feel like I just had a stroke," she said, glancing around at the diminished lighting, her first words in ten minutes. "You know, someday the lights will dim, and it won't be because lunch is changing to dinner." She looked him in the eye and said. "Someday the lights will dim because someday we'll die."

Politely as he could, he told her that he would be skipping dessert.

Dog Attack

This morning when Dustin was out walking his beagle, Princess, the darned little thing started to talk bad about Dustin's wife. One minute she was tugging on the leash and rooting in the dirt and pooping on the sidewalk like a normal dog, and the next she turned around and glared up at him and started ranting.

"I've got something to say, and you just better listen, mister," she growled in her throaty dog voice. "Just yesterday her highness neglected to give me a treat when I did that retarded trick she's always begging for. And she hasn't taken me for a walk in weeks. Can she get off her big butt and cut the web surfing down to five hours a day? And I'm not even going to mention the blanket in my crate. Pee-yew! Doesn't she know how the washing machine works? I gotta tell you man, how you put up with her, I have no idea."

"Hey, that's not fair, and you know it!" Dustin shouted, caught off guard by this tirade.

But by then Princess was pretending to be fascinated by a squirrel scampering up a nearby tree. A young couple pushing a baby carriage gave Dustin a strange look and hurried by, keeping as much of the sidewalk between themselves and Dustin as they could.

Dustin yanked the leash, pulling Princess away from the squirrel, and they resumed walking—but the walk was no longer fun for either of them. A great deal of unspoken tension hung in the air all the way home.

When they arrived at the back door, they could hear Dustin's wife moving around in the living room. As Dustin unhooked the leash from Princess's collar, he bent close to Princess's big stupid floppy ears and whispered with as much dignity as he could project, "We'll discuss this later."

Does this Hurt?

"Does this hurt?" she asked.

The physical therapist had one hand on the back of Bill's thigh and the other grasped around his ankle. She pushed the ankle toward his butt, encountering resistance even though she wasn't even close to a ninety-degree angle.

Bill's face pressed into the naughahyde-covered table. His glasses jutted halfway off his face, smashed into the bridge of his nose, and poked into his left eyeball. The naughahyde smelled exactly like the cheap, inflatable wading pool he had splashed around in as a kid.

"Does this hurt?" she asked again, a little louder this time, while forcing his knee an excruciating inch farther.

Bill's lips had become vacuum-sealed to the naughahyde, so he rolled his head a bit to the right to free up his mouth in an attempt to answer her. There was a little suction "pop" when his mouth disengaged the table. But even with his mouth now open, the only sound that escaped was a faint gasp.

She pushed his leg another inch. He could actually hear unidentified fleshy material inside his knee tearing.

"Bill?" she asked once more, very loud and clear this time. *"Does this hurt?"*

He really wanted to answer. The physical therapist was an intelligent, nice person who went out of her way to be pleasant company during these difficult sessions. Bill wanted to summon a calm voice to pronounce the word "yes" with clarity and dignity. He didn't want to remain silent and unresponsive, but his wide-open mouth just wouldn't form a coherent word.

When Bill finally managed to get sound to make its way up from his throat and out into the world, he screamed like a five-year-old whose mean older brother had just ripped the legs off his favorite G.I. Joe.

Middle-Aged Superhero Superpowers List

1) Can identify even obscure celebrity voice-overs in TV commercials.

2) Can read difficult books even in dim light.

3) Can always, always, put commas in correct places.

4) Can spot ~~blatently~~ blatantly misspelled words in oddball short story collections.

5) Can overeat at lunch and then do so again at dinner even after a big breakfast.

6) Can determine just by smell if milk in the back of the fridge has gone bad.

7) Can correctly use affect and effect; accept and except; there, their, and they're.

8) Can program his cell phone, usually, at least the simple functions.

9) Can toss his shirt in the dryer for ten minutes to remove wrinkles without ironing.

10) Can tell amusing anecdotes without using the "F-word."

11) Can look into nearly direct sunlight and only squint a little while wearing sunglasses.

12) Can hold back intestinal gas during job interviews.

13) Can lick envelope seal without cutting his tongue, usually.

14) Can win a footrace against his four-year-old niece if given proper time to train and warm up.

15) Can cut his own hair.

16) Can get laundry acceptably clean without separating whites from colors.

17) Can return bent paper clip to usable shape with only his bare hands and pliers.

18) Can pay bills before final notice arrives in the mail, but only near the beginning of the month.

19) Can see badly dressed teenagers and withhold comment.

20) Can realize that he has never been and never will be a superhero.

Change!!!

This morning as Wanda touched the snooze alarm for the fourth time, she felt a piece of notepaper on top of the alarm clock. When she pulled it close to her squinting eyes, she read the word "Change!!!" underlined three times. The handwriting was hers, but she didn't remember writing it—must have been one of those twilight zone half-awake half-asleep messages. She racked her brain for a few seconds but just couldn't figure out what she had been trying to tell herself with that one word so forcefully underlined and marked with three exclamation points.

Was it something simple and practical, such as changing the time on her alarm clock so that she didn't have to use the snooze function so often?

Perhaps it was more to the root of the problem—admonishing herself to get to bed earlier each night.

Or was it more global? Did she mean that she should look for a new line of work or simply try to do a better job in her current position?

Should she finally develop some better eating habits or drink those eight servings of water that she knew she should be getting each day?

Was she telling herself to break the cycle of getting involved with a series of attractive but selfish and ultimately destructive men?

Maybe she should get back into therapy to discover what she really needed to change.

By the time her alarm went off again after the seven-minute snooze cycle, she decided to give up. She had to drag herself to the shower and start another day. She could postpone further self-examination for her lunch hour.

As Wanda staggered through the living room toward the bathroom, she glanced at the coffee table. There she saw a bag of coin wrappers alongside an enormous pile of pennies, nickels, dimes, and quarters that she had finally remembered to bring in from her car last night.

Renovations

Stuart's building always seemed to be undergoing an endless series of updates to keep it from falling down around the people inside. The only event that happened more often than a renovation was another seminar on customer satisfaction. Stuart had been to five such seminars in the past month alone.

The most recent construction project involved tearing apart every restroom in the place—except for the one that was kept open so that no one had to run to the gas station down the street when the time came to do one's business. Supposedly the finished restrooms would be state-of-the-art when they got completed in about six months, but for now, they were useless.

Tonight, as Stuart walked back to his office, a guy he had never seen before stood outside one of the gutted, doorless men's rooms near the back of the building. Stuart thought he might be a messenger or even a new custodian, but he couldn't be sure. Just because he wore ratty cargo pants, sneakers, and a baseball cap didn't mean he couldn't be the owner of a copy shop or a coffee bar. These days, Stuart could never tell.

The guy stared wide-eyed into the empty room with its bare floors and walls. The room's only features were a few useless pipe stumps sticking out of the walls about a foot off the floor. The guy must have heard Stuart's footsteps because he spoke without pulling his gaze from the restroom.

"Dude," he said, wagging his head sideways in Stuart's direction. "Dude, come look at this."

Stuart stopped beside him and looked into the room.

"Tell me something," the guy said. "Did there used to be toilets in here?"

"Yes," Stuart answered. "The restrooms are being renovated."

"Cool!" the guy replied, breaking into a relieved smile. "I was sure there were toilets in here before. Thanks, dude!"

"You're welcome," Stuart replied, then turned and walked toward his office, happy that at the next seminar, he could report another satisfied customer.

Bond

The drinking fountain near the basketball court was out of order, so between games, Stan and Wes walked down to the fountain by the racquetball courts. Their team had won, so they didn't have much to say. When they lose, they talk more.

A game of wallyball was in progress when they got to the fountain. It's like volleyball, only the net is hung across the middle of the racquetball court, and the ball can be played off the walls—hence the name.

Stan and Wes watched the game for a few seconds. The wallyball guys didn't seem that much different from the ones in their basketball game—similar shoes, shorts, shirts. But something was a bit *off* about this whole wallyball thing. Hard to put a finger on what it was, but something was strange.

The wallyball game broke up as Stan and Wes finished their drinks, and the players came out for drinks of their own.

"You guys want to play?" one of them asked.

"No thanks," Stan and Wes replied politely in unison and turned to walk back to the basketball court.

Maybe it was because they didn't know these guys. Maybe they were afraid of looking bad at a game they'd never played before. Maybe it was loyalty to their chosen sport.

Neither of them could shake the weird feeling. Stan could tell Wes felt it too. Stan had never seen Wes away from the gym in the five years they'd played basketball together. He vaguely remembered that Wes had once mentioned that he was an accountant, but he wasn't sure. Maybe he said underwriter, whatever that was. If Stan saw Wes on the street wearing slacks, long sleeves, and a tie, he didn't think he'd recognize him.

Wes nudged Stan with his elbow when they reached the basketball court.

"Hey Stan," he said in a low voice. "If you ever come here and see me playing wallyball ... just shoot me right then.

Okay?"

"I will if you promise to do the same for me," Wes replied.

They didn't even need to shake hands to seal the deal.

The First Five Pages

When Jack was twenty-three years old and imagining himself to be a writer, he met Kurt Vonnegut. Vonnegut was an author so famous that he really had no business giving a lecture at the second-rate graduate school where Jack skipped classes in Colonial American Poetry and Deconstructionist Literary Theory to read 1950s science fiction novels and scratch out short stories for hours at a time in the window booth of the pizza place on Main Street while trying to build the nerve to smile at the pretty college girls who sat nearby.

The day after Vonnegut's lecture, as Jack sat in that pizza place among all those pretty girls who had no idea who Kurt Vonnegut was, Vonnegut himself walked in, the English department chair trailing along behind him and talking nonstop long after the great author had ceased listening politely.

Jack had trouble smiling at pretty girls, but he knew a pivotal moment when he saw one. He walked right by that befuddled department chair and pushed a heap of paper toward Vonnegut, the only famous writer Jack had ever seen in the flesh.

"Would you read my story, Mr. Vonnegut?" Jack asked, looking directly into the great man's face. Vonnegut took the story without hesitation, methodically counted out the first five pages like a cash register kid counting change on his first day of work, gripped them tightly, ripped them away from the staple with one clean pull, and handed them back to Jack.

With a look of grandfatherly patience, Vonnegut said, "You keep these. At your age, the first five pages just say, 'Hey, look at me. I'm a nice person writing a story.'"

Vonnegut patted Jack's shoulder as he stared at him, those first five pages drooping in Jack's sweaty hand.

The department chair gave Jack a dirty look that Jack didn't notice. Vonnegut folded the rest of Jack's story and stuck it in his back pocket as he walked away. "If I like this, I'll find out who you are," he said with a wave, "and you'll hear from me."

That was thirty years ago. Jack never heard a word.

(Kurt Vonnegut, 1922-2007)

157

He was standing in line at the theater because it seemed like a good night for a movie. Everyone else in line was paired off and holding hands, he noticed, except a pretty young blonde woman, a college student maybe, moving from couple to couple with a survey of some kind.

He was killing time and thinking about nothing in particular, watching the woman with the survey, when he realized that this was the 157th movie in a row that he had gone to alone. He wondered for a moment if a limit had been established, an allotment of times that a person can go to a movie alone before something has to be done about it. It was an odd question, one that hadn't occurred to him before, but the woman with the survey—no, actually, he realized it was a petition—was so interesting that he didn't bother to ponder any further.

The couples in line were very receptive to the woman with the petition. They listened politely, then smiled and signed their names—first one partner, then the other. Then each gave the other a smile and almost-embarrassed-to-be-doing-it-in-public kiss on the cheek.

After a few moments of smiling, signing, kissing, moving on, she worked her way along the line to him and looked him in the eye for a few long seconds. She seemed pleasant enough, friendly and attractive, so he was considering asking if she had seen the movie when she spoke.

"156."

"Excuse me," he replied.

"It's 156," she repeated. "Would you sign this please?"

"What is it?" he asked.

"It's a petition for your death," she said, pointing. "Sign right here on this line."

"Oh," he said, took her pen, just barely brushing the skin of her fingers as he did, and signed his name.

"Come with me," she said, taking him by the hand and pulling him ahead in the line as the other couples stepped aside to let them through. "It's a love story."

"What?" he asked.

"The movie, silly" she said. "It's a love story. They're saving the best seats for us."

Tests

Everything with this woman felt like a test.

If she cooked dinner, she'd study his face as he ate the first bite—not as if she were thinking, *I hope he likes my baked chicken,* but more like, *If he doesn't like my baked chicken, then he doesn't really love me.* If he cooked dinner, she tasted everything very tentatively. *If I don't like his broiled salmon, then he doesn't really love me.*

Things went like that, like a series of tests: calling the day after a date, selecting a video to rent, going out alone or with friends, channel surfing on the couch, staying overnight or going home to get up early for work, touching which body part and by whom and in what order when making love. Often they managed to have a good time together, but sometimes it seemed like one test after another.

He must have passed most of the tests because, eventually, the relationship got serious. They picked an apartment together, which turned out to be a whole series of tests. Whose stereo would be set up in the living room and whose in the bedroom? Whose pictures got hung on which walls? Where would the shampoo be placed in the shower? Who wanted which side of the bed? Would the bathroom door be locked, pulled shut, cracked a little, or all the way open during which grooming ritual or bodily function?

He loved her and wanted her to know that he did, so he really worked at passing her tests. He spent most of his time developing a mindset that could prepare him ahead of time for any test. The key to passing was simply giving in to her or making sure that she always got whatever was first, biggest, best, easiest, most stimulating, longest lasting, or highest paying. He figured that the correct answer to every test question was pleasing her.

The ultimate test came on the day over breakfast (she got the last of the jam for her English muffin) when she casually said, "Maybe we should get married soon." Six weeks later, they did. Another test passed with honors.

The marriage, on the other hand, was the first test he failed. It took him ten years of frequent re-tests and make-up exams, but he failed it as badly as a freshman who parties until dawn every day of finals week.

New Friends

Tom eased to a stop at the traffic light just behind a "short bus"—the kind that usually carries children with "special needs." One of the kids in the back seat turned to look out the rear window. The kid's expression seemed blank and distant. Tom knew these kids are often teased or ridiculed or just ignored, so he wanted to be friendly. He lifted a hand, waved, and smiled.

The kid's face instantly transformed into a smile, and Tom noticed that the boy was older than he had originally thought—maybe high school age. The kid waved back. Then he turned to the other kids on the bus and motioned for them to come to his window.

Tom was surprised to see that all the kids on the bus were male and at least as old as the first one. In fact, most of them looked like they could use a shave with a fresh blade.

And they all waved enthusiastically, maybe even a bit manically.

Tom noticed then that this bus wasn't the bright yellow usually associated with school children. It was a dull gray—putty would be a good word for it. That word could also describe the identical uniforms worn by all the guys in the bus.

About eight or nine of them crowded around the back windows, waving and laughing. The traffic light stayed stubbornly red for a long moment. Tom stopped waving and just sort of stared at the kids, trying to figure out what exactly was happening.

Then a couple of them started shaking their fists. A few more gave Tom the finger. One of them made a gesture Tom didn't understand that involved moving his curled hand to and from his open mouth and pushing his tongue against the inside of his cheek. Tom didn't like the look of things. He checked to make sure his doors were locked. He gripped the gearshift. He pretended to fiddle with the radio even though it wasn't on.

At last, the light changed. The bus was turning right, the same direction Tom needed to turn to go home. Instead, he continued on straight through the intersection even though that meant going five minutes out of his way to get back on the right track.

As the bus turned, Tom ventured one last glance. The guys had apparently lost interest, and he could see them turning away. Tom caught just a glimpse of the brown lettering on the gray side of the bus before it passed from view. It said "Dunlow." *What the hell is "Dunlow"?* Tom wondered.

But then it hit him. "Dunlow" is the name of the prison on the outskirts of town.

Contributors to the Current Issue of _Pretty Damn Good Poetry Journal_

Suzie-Anne McWorstershire is a part-time composition teacher at Mohegan Sun Junior College in Uncasville, Connecticut. She is the author of twelve unpublished novels and a writer's guidebook, _How to Write and Publish Your Novel_, for which she is currently seeking a publisher.

Rock Stark is a photographer from Idaho who sells hunting knives at a kiosk in the Boise Mall. He is on staff at _Killdeer Magazine_.

Bradley Brady is director of the Ph.D. program in creative writing at Minnesota Oceanic University. This is his first publication.

Karen Jones is a full-time mother of three who writes erotica between four and six in the morning.

Van Clavicle is the author of _The Complete Idiot's Guide to Writing Books for Dummies_.

Gunthar Spackle teaches pilates at the Evergreen Nursing Home in Racine, Wisconsin.

Ron Turneck lives in a cabin in northern Alaska where he writes travel essays, video game instruction booklets, and anti-technology manifestoes.

Betty Roberts has been a nurse for twenty-three years. Her one-act play, "Four Out of Five Doctors are Jerks," premiered at the Woohawken Playwright's Festival last year.

Annette Overbeck is a poet and co-editor of the literary e-zine *pocketlocket.com*. Her pudding sculptures are on display at the Sub-Zero Gallery in Phoenix, Arizona.

Lynnette Lifshintoning has published 432 books of poetry, most recently, *Collected Works: August 14, 2010, 3:15 to 4:45 p.m.*

Dudley Kingsmuffin studies poetry at the Colorado Graduate School of Culinary Arts. His work has previously appeared in *Runty Sprout*, *Gravy Wave*, and *Digestion Digest*.

The estate of Mildred Kennison writes, "These poems were found under Grandma's pillow in her own handwriting. If you publish them, are they worth any money yet, or does she have to be dead longer?"

His Basketball Nicknames
from Birth to Age Forty-Five

Birth: The Next Michael Jordan
Age 1: Poopie Diaper
Age 2: Dribbler
Age 3: Mr. Snappy
Age 4: Tinkler
Age 5: Po (as in, "he has 'po'-tential")
Age 6: Chubbs
Age 7: Lumpy
Age 8: Big Train
Age 9: Groan (as in, "he has finally 'groan' into his weight")
Age 10: Floppy
Age 11: Skinny Butt
Age 12: Spaghetti Arms
Age 13: Statue (as in, "hands of stone")
Age 14: Big Hair
Age 15: No-No (as in, "'no, no,' please don't shoot the ball")
Age 16: Clunker
Age 17: Johnny Jump-Up
Age 18: Cow (as in, "he jumps over the moon")
Age 19: Luke (as in, "Skywalker")
Age 20: Air
Age 21: Fly
Age 22: Leper (as in, "nobody can touch him")
Age 23: White Lightning
Age 24: El Diablo
Age 25: Sprain
Age 26: Sir Limps-a-Lot
Age 27: Knee-Be-Gone
Age 28: Sloppy Arthroscopy
Age 29: Long Time (as in, "no see")
Age 30: Crutch

Age 31: Comeback Kid
Age 32: Rain (as in, "his jump shot brings rain")
Age 33: Gunner
Age 34: Duck (as in, "held together by 'duck' tape")
Age 35: Coach
Age 36: Day (as in, "back in the 'day,' he once could play")
Age 37: Old School
Age 38: Pappy
Age 39: Viagra
Age 40: The Distinguished Gentleman from Massachusetts
Age 41: Whitey White Hair
Age 42: Jo-Jo, Jumps-Too Low, Runs-Too-Slow
Age 43: One Room (as in, "so old school the school only had 'one room'")
Age 44: Frank (as in, "Frank N. Stein")
Age 45: Florida (as in, "retired")

Authorship

She had written one book, which was published in her early twenties. The reviews were strong and the sales began briskly before leveling off. It was a really good book full of love and life and really nice syntax. But it was only one book, and she wasn't sure how to start a second one.

A few years after the book got backlisted, she married a man who had written many books, mystery novels. They were pretty good books, but nothing that changed the lives of the people who read them. No one tossed his books in the garbage, but not too many re-read them either. They were married for five years and ended things on pretty good terms.

Then she met and married a man who had written many thin books of English-language versions of the ancient Japanese poetic forms haiku, senryu, and tanka. He wasn't a traditionalist who counted syllables. He tried for moments of intuition and emotional insight in his little poems. People would nod and say "ah" at his poetry readings, and he won a couple of minor awards. But he couldn't get a tenure-track university position, which made his poetry take on a very dark tone. That marriage lasted two years. The last she heard, he had turned to writing sonnets.

A much older man, an editor at the publishing house that put out her book years before, called her one day out of the blue to see if she would have drinks with him. He had just dumped his wife of thirty years, bought a sports car, dyed his hair, and started writing screenplays about alien invasions. She met him for drinks and then for dinner the next evening. The following day, he emailed her a ten-page critique of her book. He called it a "love gift." Her return email informed him that there would be no third date.

She pretty much decided to give up on romance and joined a writing group at the local community college to see if she had another book inside her trying to make its way out. She wasn't looking to meet anyone, but she struck up a conversation one night with a man in the group who had been working on the same short story for nearly two decades. It was his first story, and he started writing it years ago not long after he read her book, which still occupied an honored place on his desk in the fourth-grade classroom where he taught learning-disabled students to read better every day from 8 a.m. to 4 p.m. At lunch, after school, and on weekends when he wasn't volunteering for a local conservation group, he worked on his story, tinkering with the sentences and trying to discover the protagonist's true motivation.

They've been married now for more than twenty years. She just published her seventh novel, all bestsellers, including the reissue of her first, and he has read each one several times. All seven were on his desk right up until the day he retired from teaching. He now has more time for fine-tuning the end of that one short story. He promises she can take a look at it someday—just as soon as he finishes.

Compound-Word Adjectives

"We learned something really interesting in English class today," Lynnette told her husband Hugo over the crock-pot chili she had made for dinner. "Professor Madgek told us that compound-word adjectives are groups of two or more words that come directly before the noun they modify." She leaned toward Hugo and pulled down the corner of his sports section. "Here's the interesting part—you have to use a hyphen when the compound-word adjective comes *directly* before the noun, but not if it isn't directly before the noun."

Hugo looked up from the basketball box-score reports and stared at her.

"Yeah?" he said. "You think that's interesting? Is that the kind of useless-ass crap you're learning at that fancy-pants community college? I hated English in high school, and I got negative-zero interest in hearing about it now."

Lynnette dropped the corner of the paper, which floated down into Hugo's half-eaten bowl of chili.

"Here's another thing about that college," Hugo continued. "If your smarty-smart Professor Madgek knows so much, why ain't he teaching at the state university instead of misfit-toys community college for brain-damaged teenagers and washed-up, middle-aged housewives?"

Lynnette glared. "For your information, Professor Madgek is very smart. He used to teach at a university in the Midwest, but he likes community colleges better. He said it's a community-outreach thing for him, make the world a better place by providing learner-centered education in a nurture-based environment."

"Sounds like he missed his life-long calling," Hugo replied, wiping chili from the point-spread listings for this weekend's football games. "He ought to be a bleeding-heart nursemaid instead of a professor."

Lynnette grabbed Hugo's bowl and dropped it into the

sink with her own. Hugo didn't notice the nerve-jangling clang as he kept talking in his cringe-inducing voice.

"You know what? Your precious Professor Madgek seems like a pansy-ass fruitcake, if you ask me. He spends his whole day running off at the mouth about adjectives and poetry—that sounds pretty queer-ball homo to me."

Lynnette rinsed the chili residue from the bowls and rubbed them hard with the scratchy soap pad. She resisted a near-overwhelming urge to break one of the bowls over Hugo's suitcase-sized head as he left the table, carrying the sports section to the upstairs bathroom for his nightly half-hour, post-dinner session on the toilet.

While she dried her hands on the flower-bordered towel, she thought of how she rubbed those same hands over Professor Madgek's rock-hard abdominal muscles that afternoon in his office after class. He had kissed her with that heat-probing tongue of his that always made her head spin. Pansy-ass fruitcake? Lynnette chuckled. Queer-ball homo? Not hardly.

Then she thought of the new ingredient she had added to Hugo's chili just before she served it to him: *Detection-proof poison.*

Breakfast

One of the drawbacks to the area where Roger lives is that there aren't many good breakfast places. Sure, there's a McDonald's, and that's okay when he's in a hurry and only interested in breakfast on the run. And there's Denny's and Friendly's, interchangeable places where they usually neglect to scrape the onions off the grill before they apply the pancake batter. No amount of syrup can mitigate the taste of an onion-flavored pancake.

So Roger was thrilled when a new breakfast place opened a couple of towns over.

He likes bringing a selection of books to satisfy his reading appetite while he eats. The server takes his order and delivers a big stack of non-onion-flavored pancakes with a little bottle of blueberry syrup, two sausage patties, two thick-sliced slabs of country bacon, and two biscuits slathered in butter and jam. This is sometimes Roger's only meal of the day. Through the afternoon and evening, he might snack on apples, carrots, and rice cakes as penance for his sinful but delectable breakfast.

He goes there two or three mornings a week for a couple hours before heading to work. Breakfast is the most important meal of the day, as the saying goes. And for a spartan like Roger, it's also one of his few indulgences—shelves filled with books and mornings filled with big breakfasts.

Recently, Brenda, a cashier at the new breakfast place, started flirting with Roger. She spots him reading and comes over to say hi and ask about that day's book. She's bright, friendly, and very pretty, with a smile like perfectly fried egg whites and enough self-confidence not to dye the sexy beginnings of gray in her bobbed black hair.

Roger and Brenda talk about books and school and movies, plus a few personal subjects. Roger has discovered that they have a lot in common. They're both divorced, childless, about the same age, and living in small apartments in towns five miles apart. So when she flirts, Roger can't help but think, *Hey, why not?* and flirt back.

But then Roger thinks about his history. He has two ex-wives and about a dozen ex-girlfriends going back twenty years. All of them have been bright, pretty, and appealing in so many different ways. Some have been deep, some shallow. Some have left huge voids in his life, some just relief. He remembers all their names, and he's pretty sure some still think of him. A few probably hate him, but a few still call once in a while and think of him as a friend.

The other day, Brenda was clearly hinting about going to a movie that weekend. Roger could be kind of dense about these things, but he understood flirting well enough to know that she was opening a door for him to walk through with an invitation to sit close together in the dark at whatever might be playing at the multiplex down the road from the breakfast place.

For most of his life, he would have happily walked through that open door, thrilled to spend time in the company of someone like Brenda, an intelligent, attractive, available woman who clearly wanted his company. The possibilities for where this date might lead were endless and appealing—first date, second date, third, fourth, girlfriend, lover, fiancée, wife.

Or ex-wife. Or just ex-girlfriend. Maybe they would stay friends, or maybe she'd curse him to hell.

Maybe Roger is getting old. It's a door he decided not to pass through this time. Sure, Brenda is terrific. But Roger has come to the decision that there are probably hundreds of terrific women in this town, but there's only one terrific breakfast place.

Faking It

The call came at 7:30, exploding Jack from Saturday morning sleep. It was the admission director at the community college where Jack teaches.

"Monica was going to talk about careers in the liberal arts, but she called in sick. Twenty people signed up. It starts in half an hour. Can you do it?"

Jack agreed, silently cursed his colleague Monica, gobbled some toast, ducked in and out of the shower, dragged a toothbrush through his mouth, put on a necktie, and raced to the college.

This was a recruiting program to attract new students. They mainly came from the technical high schools in the area. These were kids who either didn't like or had trouble with the traditional academic program. They were the bread and butter, the ones who weren't going to big state universities or small, selective colleges. Open enrollment, minuscule tuition, and practical programs attracted them.

Today's event included introductions to such programs as accounting, computer repair, office administration, and machine technology, among the many other job-preparation areas of the curriculum. The "Careers in the Liberal Arts" session Jack was drafted to chair stood out like a sore thumb that also had a broken nail painted pink.

He had a hard time believing that twenty people would sign up for such an oxymoron. Perhaps they were late registrants closed out of the "real" sessions. Maybe they were just confused. Jack certainly was.

When he walked into the room, there were indeed twenty young people staring at him, waiting for him to enlighten them for the next hour. In the back corner sat two of their teachers in jeans and sweatshirts, looking as content as if they had just taken a break from tending their vegetable gardens to pop in for a visit.

Jack killed about ten minutes rambling about the college in general: small class size, great parking, and caring staff. Then he spent fifteen minutes trying to define the indefinite. Just what the hell is "liberal arts" anyway? He couldn't help thinking that his explanation only managed to confuse them (and himself) even more.

He asked them what careers they were interested in. One young man raised his hand and said, "H-VAC." Ignorance and embarrassment were now added to Jack's confusion when he had to ask him what "H-VAC" was. "Heating, ventilation, and air conditioning," the kid told him without a trace of condescension. No one else volunteered a career choice.

Another five minutes gone—although Jack honestly believed that the clock on the classroom wall actually started ticking backward.

Finally, Jack turned to what he knew best: writing, critical thinking, communications. "You'll all have to write reports for your jobs, give presentations to clients," he said. "Employers want people who can work together and think creatively, not just do what they're told."

That took ten minutes. Then he asked for their questions. "Sorry," Jack responded, "but we don't have any sports teams."

Jack let them go ten minutes before the hour was up. Giving them plenty of time to get to their next session was his excuse, but they knew he had nothing left to say. They gave him a spattering of polite applause before leaving anyway.

As everyone filed out, the two teachers beamed at Jack. They clapped his shoulders and pumped his hand, happy, it seemed, not to be the ones faking it for a change.

A Few Questions Regarding the Supreme Court's "Corporate Personhood" Decision

1) If a person creates a corporation, does that make that person God?

2) If a person incorporates himself or herself and becomes both a person and a corporation, does that mean that person suffers from Schizophrenia?

3) Can people take out restraining orders against those annoying corporations that constantly harass them with telemarketing calls?

4) If those shady military corporations are persons, and one of them is captured by the enemy, can it be waterboarded, and, if so, does that constitute torture?

5) If the McDonald's and Burger King corporations merged, is that a same-sex marriage?

6) If a corporation has First Amendment rights, does that also mean it has Second Amendment rights to arm itself?

7) If a corporation breaks a "three-strikes" law three times, shouldn't it be put in prison forever?

8) Is corporate bankruptcy suicide?

9) Is a corporate takeover by another corporation murder?

10) If a corporation is convicted of murder in a death penalty state, how should it be executed?

11) Are multinational corporations citizens of the United States, or are they illegal immigrants?

12) If a corporation commits a crime before it has existed for eighteen years, are the juvenile court records kept secret?

13) If a prison corporation is convicted of a crime, can it serve its sentence inside itself?

14) If a corporation goes out of business before embracing Jesus as its personal savior, would the television evangelists claim that its soul is damned to the fires of hell for all eternity?

15) If a corporation is a person, isn't owning stock in a corporation a form of slave owning?

16) Is a corporation subject to compulsory education laws until age 16?

17) Should a corporation have to wait until it has existed for eighteen years before it can participate in elections?

18) If a corporation is a person, shouldn't all of its employees together have only one vote?

19) If a corporation is a person, shouldn't all corporations get immediate psychological counseling?

20) Should a corporate board of directors include an id, an ego, and a superego?

21) If a mortgage company is a person, would it be socially awkward if its credit rating dipped too low to qualify for a mortgage from itself?

22) Can a corporation run for office, and, if that corporation wins, can it be impeached when it screws every working person in America?

23) Can a corporation just eliminate the middleman and actually get itself appointed to the Supreme Court by the next Republican President?

24) Is there a corporation in America confused and ignorant enough to join the Tea Party and not realize that the whole "movement" is a corporation-funded sham?

25) If a corporation is a person and registers to vote as a Republican, isn't that just redundant?

26) If money equals speech, then why doesn't every person have as much money as every corporation?

27) Where exactly is a corporation's ass because there are quite a few that would benefit from a good, swift, hard kick there?

Letter to Santa

1 December 2010

Santa Claus, President
Christmastime Productions
1 Pole Place
North Pole 00000

Dear Mr. Claus,

This letter is in response to the lump of coal received by stocking just before midnight, 24 December 2009, to be forwarded to my eight-year-old son, Johnny Jr., on Christmas morning, 2009. Said coal was an entirely inappropriate gift for Johnny Jr. I know you have been in this business a long time, and you are an "expert" in your "field," but I must submit my deepest objection to your position (as expressed in your handwritten note accompanying the coal) that Johnny Jr. had been a "very, very bad boy" during the calendar year 2009.

While it is true that Johnny had some attitude problems relating to his little sister Paige, he has since worked out those problems with the help of his therapist. This year, we have had no repeats of the unfortunate bathtub, skating rink, or backyard mudslide incidents that occurred in 2009. (Paige is healing nicely and sends her thanks for the My Little Pony Hospital Set you provided for her last Christmas.)

I must also mention that the investigators have informed us that electrical issues might have been just as likely the cause of this October's fire as Johnny's recreational use of kitchen matches. Unfortunately, it will be necessary this year to forward whatever presents might be headed our way to my brother-in-law Stan Frankel's home in Parsippany, New Jersey, because the repairs to our house will not be finished until February.

In Johnny's favor is his exemplary work in school, where he is making wonderful progress and will almost surely complete the first grade on this year's attempt. In addition, we are confident that he will once again be allowed to enjoy recess with his classmates before the snows have melted this spring. Johnny has also been a big help to his mother, my lovely wife Julie (thanks from her for the *Prevention Magazine* subscription!). The doctors tell us that I will only need to be on this liquid diet for another few weeks, once the effects of the food poisoning from Johnny's Thanksgiving dinner "help" have worn off. (As a related aside here, I would really appreciate a new blender for Christmas—Stan's is in very poor condition.)

So I hope you can agree that no one wants to repeat last year's coal incident this holiday season. Perhaps instead, this year you might provide more games to go with the X-Box 360 I procured for Johnny last year shortly after I discovered the coal in his stocking. (It was wonderful timing to find those nice men selling electronic equipment from the trunk of their car downtown on Christmas morning. Do I sense your miracle-working hand in this serendipity?) FYI: Johnny is especially fond of games with lots of violence and bloodshed, and I am thankful that he has this cathartic outlet for his occasional aggressive tendencies.

Warmest holiday wishes,

John Kringle

John Kringle

Child of the Decade
Award Acceptance Speech,
December 31, 1969

Thank you, ladies and gentlemen. It is with humility and gratitude that I accept this Child of the Decade Award. The 1960s were a turbulent time in our nation's history, a time when we all awakened to the possibilities of life beyond racism, sexism, and classism. I am very, very thankful that my small example as Child of the Decade contributed to this history-making era.

My journey began shortly after the Pittsburgh Pirates clinched the National League pennant in the fall of 1960. My heartfelt thanks go out to the Pirates' players, managers, and team officials for inspiring my father and mother to celebrate their achievement by conceiving me. The team's subsequent World Series victory helped to keep my parents' marriage happy and provide me with a stable home for years to come.

I would also like to thank my twin brother for his companionship during those gestational months together. Our telepathic conversations and shared memories of the origin of the human species were an endless source of encouragement, enlightenment, and delight. I can only hope that our time together contributed in some small way to his ascendancy to president of his class at Winslow Elementary School, the youngest third-grader to hold such office.

The many teachers who have given of their time and energy to guide my education deserve so much more than my meager thank-yous. Without their support, my eighteen weeks of public school, six months of college, and two years for combined medical and legal degrees at Yale University would have taken much longer and delayed my path in life. We are all learners, but these people with great minds and hearts and spirits, I am proud to call my teachers.

I would be unforgivably remiss if I did not mention the many wonderful men and women of the Professional Bowlers Association who gladly granted me an age exception so that I could tour the great cities of America and pursue my passion for the pins. Although it is not enough to show my gratitude, I would like to donate my $800,000 prize money from this year's tournaments to the Kegglers Against Cancer Fund.

To the editors of all the magazines, newspapers, and anthologies that have printed my early scrawlings, I send my thanks for your support and encouragement. To everyone at Doubleday who helped me realize a new dream with the publication of each of my seven novels, four short story collections, seven books of essays, and twelve volumes of poetry, and to the great people at Oxford University Press for championing my textbooks on physics, organic chemistry, prosody, and social theory—what can I say? Thank you so much.

My appreciation also goes out to President Richard Nixon for inviting me to the White House so many times. You have often told me how much my counsel has meant to you as you perform the duties of your esteemed office, but I pray that I have shown a fraction of the guidance that you have provided me. I only wish we had kept some kind of recording of our many conversations on foreign and domestic policy to enlighten future generations.

Tomorrow, as I meet with leaders from around the globe at the World Conference on Peace and Prosperity for the 1970s, I will do everything that I can to live up to the honor bestowed upon me this evening. Perhaps if we can all come together and show one another the same care and commitment that my parents gave to me through these nearly nine wonderful years, the coming decade will indeed be one that brings the world together.

Thanks Mom and Dad. I love you!

Thirty-Nine Random, Inappropriate Thoughts at a Funeral

1) It was just a couple of times back in college, kind of experimental. It doesn't make me gay.

2) Wow, look at her! She's my third cousin, I think. That's distant enough.

3) I can't be the only person who thinks the *Harry Potter* movies were better than the *Lord of the Rings* series.

4) It's been a month. How long does it take for the god-damned Prozac to kick in?

5) My butt hurts.

6) If I keep putting the underwear that I've just washed into the top of my underwear drawer, then those will be the first ones I grab to wear, and they will wear out a lot faster than the ones at the bottom of the drawer. I need to start a rotating system before any real damage is done.

7) They couldn't have spent very much on that ugly coffin.

8) I'd have to live to be 300 to pay back all of my student loans.

9) He slept with her and her and her and her and probably her and maybe her.

10) I just went half an hour ago. I can't believe I have to go again.

11) Mental note: Next time, take the porno out of the DVD player before my wife gets home from work.

12) This minister looks like one of those evil priests from a Stephen King movie.

13) Just sit right back and you'll hear a tale, a tale of a fateful trip, that started from this tropic port, aboard this tiny ship.

14) I know we were married for ten years, but I just didn't feel like saying hi to her today. Is that such a crime?

15) Was that a fart or someone's chair squeaking?

16) Man, that guy must have put on eighty pounds since high

school.

17) If the Sox's starters don't give them seven good innings every game, they're screwed with the crappy bullpen they've got this year.

18) I can't believe she's wearing white shoes in October. And I can't believe I noticed.

19) I have no idea how much she paid for those breasts, but she sure got her money's worth.

20) The Loch Ness Monster? Maybe. But Bigfoot? That's just ridiculous.

21) If I cough while I yawn, maybe no one will notice that I'm yawning.

22) Sure, they're not the biggest bunch up there, but my flowers are pretty damned impressive.

23) I hope they have those little sandwiches with the crust cut off.

24) Of course it makes a noise. How could a whole big tree fall in a forest and not make any noise?

25) What the hell is a throttle body assembly? I think that mechanic is trying to rip me off again.

26) If Ferguson thinks I'm going to protect his sorry ass when they find out about those orders he shipped to Australia, he's sadly mistaken!

27) Eight o'clock *Star Trek* re-run, Lakers versus Celtics at nine—and then hello, Spice Channel!

28) Come on, Reverend, pick up the pace a bit! We're all dying here!

29) You know, I'll bet egg whites would make my pie crusts flakier.

30) Would anybody notice if I called Domino's and had a pizza delivered?

31) Ugh! She just blew her nose on that thing, and now he's putting it back in his pocket. That can't be healthy.

32) Did I leave the iron on?

33) Whoa! Did he just move!? He couldn't have moved, dummy. He's dead.

34) Has anybody else noticed that Windows is just a bad imitation of Macintosh?

35) Dadaists, Surrealists, Cubists ... I finally see how they all fit together.

36) I actually prefer the industrial-grade toilet paper. That fluffy stuff falls apart too easily.

37) What's up with that yellow carpet stain over there?

38) He was a jerk. I'll get more people than this at my funeral.

39) Finally! Let's eat!

Suspect

Josh had been moving all weekend, filling his small truck and hauling load after load from the old apartment to his new house. As a single person in his mid-twenties, for the first time, he felt like such a grown-up, such a "real person" for having gone through all of the house-buying tasks that seemed so endless when he first walked into the bank four months ago. They gave him about a thousand pages of forms to fill out and, after countless meetings, phone calls, and credit explanation letters, he had finally been approved and closed on the mortgage for the little cape on the country lane just last week. Josh was now a homeowner—but one last step remained. He actually had to move into his new home.

Compared with a family of four, Josh didn't have much stuff, but it seemed like a lot because he was moving it all himself during a single weekend to save money. He packed all week and began moving Saturday morning at six, before the summer heat got intense, ate on the run when he could, and collapsed into bed that night at nine. He was up and working again at six Sunday morning, retracing the ten-mile route between the house and apartment again and again, looking forward to sleeping in his new house for the first time that night. In fact, his bed was the last item packed onto the truck for the last trip as late afternoon became early evening. On the way, he decided to stop at McDonald's and get a burger so that he didn't pass out from hunger.

This McDonald's had one of those playscapes that kids love. As Josh stood in line waiting to order, he watched about five children rollicking in a huge bin of plastic balls, diving out of site and emerging to scream with delight. They couldn't possibly ever have more fun in their lives than they were having right at that moment.

One mother had just finished corralling her two kids and herded them toward the exit. As they passed him, Josh couldn't help but stare. They were completely delightful—a boy and a girl, maybe a year or so apart, just a shade under three feet tall, each clad in jeans with the cuffs folded up over their tiny scale models of adult-style basketball shoes, ketchup stains on their faces and shirts. As a new homeowner, Josh thought about meeting a nice woman who would want to have kids just like these to fill their hearts and the second bedroom in the new house. He liked that thought.

Josh smiled at the kids and said hi as they paused on their way out to gaze up at him with their big, curious kids' eyes.

Their mother quickly pulled them toward the door, hissing, "Let's go ... *we don't know him.*"

Josh glanced up to see her give him a look so dirty it would wither a perennial. She glared at him her whole way to the door, then hustled the kids into a minivan and sped away. Josh had no idea what he had done to deserve such a look.

He got his burger and unwrapped it on the way to the truck, inhaling the addictive fat odor and taking the first bite. When he reached for his door handle, he got a look at his reflection in the driver-side window. Josh had to admit that he wasn't a pretty sight.

Sweat stained his armpits and actually seeped out to meet in the middle of his chest, forming a Mickey Mouse silhouette. His unwashed hair was plastered to his head. Cobwebs dangled from his beard. Scratches and bruises lined his forearms from carrying boxes, furniture, and other assorted possessions that he couldn't bring himself to toss out. His jeans were shiny from wiping sweaty palms on them.

And his zipper was down.

It wasn't just down. It was way down, down all the way and gaping open to reveal his underwear—underwear that was, Josh was ashamed to admit, sweat-stained and filthy.

Needless to say, he was horrified to be out in public looking like this. But at least he now knew why the woman had yanked her kids away from him. She must have figured he was some kind of pervert on the prowl for his next victim.

Josh quickly ducked into the privacy of his driver's seat, covered his wild hair with a hat, raked the webs from his beard, and promised himself a hot shower when he got to the new house.

As he was leaving the parking lot, a police cruiser pulled in with its lights flashing. It dawned on Josh that the woman must have called 9-1-1 from her cell phone as she was leaving McDonald's, hoping to protect other mothers' children from the wild man on the loose. The officers gave Josh a sharp-eyed look as they passed, so he nodded to them, and then dutifully engaged his turn signal, doing his best to look like the respectable, property-owning citizen he knew himself to be as he drove toward his new home and his new life.

Handsome Stranger

When Anne saw the remarkable stranger walking a dog in the park on an otherwise ordinary summer evening, she sensed that fate had arranged for this man to cross her path. Her mind could only hold one thought: *This is the most handsome man I have ever seen.*

"Hello," the handsome man said through a smile so white his teeth pulled light from the air around his mouth.

Anne could hardly believe he had spoken to her, had said the word "hello" through lips so full and perfectly shaped for kissing.

"Hello," she replied through her own lips, which were suddenly dry.

"I'm Paul," the handsome stranger said, his voice a mix of honey and cello. "I just moved in down the street."

"I'm Anne," she said, grasping handsome Paul's offered right hand, his big, soft hand that buried hers. His left hand, dangling from a thick wrist, well-muscled arm, and square shoulder, held the dog's leash. That lovely hand, Anne noticed, held no wedding ring.

"This is Bowser," handsome Paul said, nodding a square jaw darkened with thick evening whiskers toward the dog standing beside his sandaled feet.

Anne tore her eyes from Paul's handsomeness to look at the dog for the first time. Bowser was mid-sized, about two feet tall, the color of charcoal, so dusky he looked like he would darken the palms of anyone who touched him.

"Hi, Bowser," Anne said, noticing the affected lilt in her own voice. Anne wasn't a "dog person." She didn't have one as a child and had never felt the need for one as an adult. She had no interest in paying for, housing, feeding, walking, and cleaning up after such creatures. She could take them or leave them. In Anne's experience, humans made the best companions—humans like Paul, for example.

Handsome Paul was leashed to this dog at this moment, so this dog was worth the effort. Anne knelt beside Bowser, whom she now noticed was a mutt of undeterminable lineage—and not a good mix. Maybe some Lab, perhaps some dachshund, a pinch of boxer, a hint of terrier—overall, more a chunking of attributes than a true blend. He was as thick around as a beer keg with a football head, meatloaf neck, and short, spindly legs.

"I think Bowser likes you," handsome Paul said. "Don't you, Bowser?"

Bowser grunted and thrust his head at Anne. Reflexively, she put her hand on his back but had to consciously force herself not to pull away. Bowser's spine bones jutted into her palm through his wire coat. Dander dust wafted from just the light stroke she gave him.

It's not his fault, Anne thought. *He's a dog. He can't help being a little dirty. Think about how handsome Paul is. Just keep petting. Pet the dog. Think of Paul. Pet the dog. Think of Paul … handsome, handsome Paul.*

"He likes being scratched behind the ears," handsome Paul said. Anne glanced up at him. She liked the view from this angle. *Yep,* she thought, *just as handsome as he was fifteen seconds ago.*

Anne looked down at the big ears on the back of Bowser's clunky head. The skin was scabrous. Anne thought of how Paul's wavy hair was nothing like Bowser's ratty rug. She guided her fingernails lightly over the ruined, patch-furred skin just behind Bowser's right ear.

Bowser looked up to meet Anne's gaze. His right eye was ink-dark and featureless. His left was circled in a blood-red, inside-out lid. That eye bulged, nearly disconnected from the socket. Bowser eased his snout closer to Anne's face. His breath smelled like something found months too late in the back of the refrigerator, something turned green with fur growing on it. Bowser's moldy tongue lulled across one side of his jaw. Anne saw only four intact teeth, and the holes in

Bowser's gums oozed pink puss.

"Awww, he wants a kiss," handsome Paul cooed. "Bowser wants a kiss. Go ahead, Anne. Give Bowser a kiss."

At the sound of his handsome master's voice, Bowser licked the puss from his gums and dribbled a yellowish glob of phlegm to the ground. Anne had to pull her foot away to avoid the glob landing on her newly purchased walking shoes, a maneuver that nearly sent her toppling over.

Anne regained her balance and stood so quickly that Bowser and handsome Paul both backpedaled. "I just remembered something," she sputtered, striding down the sidewalk like a power-walker. "I have to be someplace for something," she called over her shoulder to Paul, his smile drooping like the sagging leash he held, like the slack skin at Bowser's four armpits.

Anne didn't look back at handsome Paul, couldn't look. She walked straight toward her echoing house—a house with no kids, no pets, no husband.

One thought filled her mind: *Nobody's that handsome.*

Mary Had a Little Phone

Mark dropped two quarters into his son Jeff's outstretched hand as the teenager finished breakfast and headed toward the door. Jeff's freshman basketball team had an away game that night.

"Give us a call from the pay phone when you get back to the school so we can pick you up," Mark said.

Jeff pocketed the coins and said with half a smile, "I wouldn't need these if I had a cell phone."

Mark gave him the dirty look Jeff expected, and they both chuckled. This scene had been repeated for nearly two years of mornings when Jeff needed to call for a ride home.

Jeff was angling for a cell phone.

Outside the kitchen window, a squirrel scampered up the pole toward the bird feeder where it encountered the large salad bowl Mark had installed upside-down halfway up the pole. Even a creature as acrobatic and gravity-defying as a squirrel wasn't going to get through Mark's salad bowl line of defense.

And Jeff wasn't going to get a cell phone.

Mark just got a cell phone for himself a year ago, long after it seemed to have been decreed by the king of the world that every peasant get one. He kept it in the glove box of his car where it would be handy in case of an accident or the inevitable traffic jam that would require the "I'm-going-to-be-late" call to home or work, depending on whether he happened to be coming or going. Accidents and traffic jams cover two-thirds of the times Mark has used his cell phone. For a while, he also checked his messages at work. That's pretty much it.

Mark has had one accident since he got the phone. He was rear-ended by an eighty-year-old woman while sitting in the Dunkin' Donuts drive-thru line. She spilled her purse and jammed on the gas when she reached down to get it, plowing into the back of Mark's car. He lent her his cell phone to call her insurance company while he rubbed his sore neck. Her insurance ended up paying for everything.

Mark had to make the "late" call maybe three times in the past year, and he stopped checking his office messages from the car about six months ago. People actually expected him to call back if he got their messages, so there really didn't seem to be a point to getting those messages early.

If pressured, Mark would have to confess that he did use the phone for one other purpose. When he first got it, he called a few friends with some *big news*.

"Hey, guess what?" he asked. "I got a cell phone." After a dramatic pause, he continued, *"And I'm talking to you on it right now."*

The friends didn't share Mark's amazement, considering most of them had owned cell phones for the better part of a decade.

"What's your number," his friends had asked, "so I can program it into my cell phone?"

"I don't know," Mark replied.

And he didn't know for weeks. He figured that if he didn't know his own number, then he couldn't tell anyone what it is, and no one would ever call him. So far, that strategy seemed to be working.

When Mark has to, he can find out what his cell number is. He devised a high-tech method for keeping it handy. He wrote it on a strip of masking tape stuck to the back of the phone.

Mark really doesn't want anyone calling him. When they call, they always seem to want something. They want Mark to do something, go somewhere, think about something, and give advice on their love lives.

And those calls are just from his friends. God forbid any telemarketers got hold of his number. He'd never get any peace.

Maybe he's old fashioned, but Mark just doesn't want the silence of his car shattered by a ringing phone. His drive time is about the only private, contemplative time in his busy day. If he wanted those cherished moments disrupted by obnoxious noise, he'd just tune in Rush Limbaugh.

Mark isn't really thrilled with the cell phone etiquette shown by the general public. For example, he was at lunch the other day when he heard a tinkling version of "Mary Had a Little Lamb" break out a few booths behind him. He recognized right away that this was a cell phone programmed to play a song rather than an old-fashioned ring like his own phone. He pictured a fourteen-year-old girl getting the call, maybe someone from his son Jeff's school—because, of course, Jeff claims to be the only person there without a cell phone.

When Mark turned around to give this teenybopper a dirty look, he saw a middle-aged businessman in a suit flipping open his phone.

"What?" the guy barked with a mouth half full of cheeseburger. "No, goddamn it! That report better be on my desk by the time I get back from lunch, or your ass is fired!"

That wasn't the kind of person Mark wants his son Jeff to become.

On his way out, Mark dropped a couple of quarters on the guy's table.

"What's that for?" the guy asked.

Mark pointed toward the pay phone on the wall by the entrance. "Next time, give Mary and her little lamb a rest."

Then Mark got in his car and dug in the glove box for his cell phone. Finally, he had discovered another use for the annoying little gizmo. He stared at it while rummaging through his mental Rolodex, trying to recall any friend's phone number because he just had to call someone to describe the look on that guy's face.

What to do When the Neighbors' Dogs Won't Stop Barking for the Thirty-Seventh Night in a Row

1) Call the "will do odd jobs" guy whose number you found on the bulletin board at the supermarket. Offer him twenty bucks. He'll know what to do.

2) Turn up the Republican National Convention really loud on the television. (This strategy won't shut up the dogs, but it will give you a new appreciation for their barking as a comparative source of intelligence in the world.)

3) Picture yourself at a peaceful beach being caressed by tranquil breezes and bathed in healing sunshine. Now picture the dogs at that same beach being chased by angry alligators.

4) Get one of those bulky suits worn by the people who train attack dogs. Smear the suit with bacon grease, put it on, and then let the dogs chew on you until they are too exhausted to bark anymore.

5) March right up to those dogs and tell them in a stern voice, "Cut it out you guys, and I mean right now."

6) Invent a soundproof fence. Install it in the appropriate location.

7) Capture your other neighbor's cat and feed it to the dogs. (This is not actually recommended, but it crosses one's mind every now and then.)

8) Go on the Internet and see if you can find one of those dog whistles everybody seemed to have when you were a kid. What the heck—anything's worth a shot.

9) Place a personal ad in the "singles" section of the newspaper. Play up the point that you are looking for someone who really, really likes dogs. (This is not recommended if you are married or in a serious, committed relationship.)

10) Tie an anonymous note to a brick and toss it through your

neighbor's window. The note should say that you "know what they're up to" and "it had better stop really soon, or there might be more bricks." (Don't mention the dogs because that would give you away.)

11) Get some sleeping pills and some water. Bring the water to a vigorous boil. Add three or four pills. Add a bouillon cube (beef or chicken—your choice). Reduce heat to medium. Cover and let simmer for half an hour. Serve at room temperature in a doggie dish.

12) Call the neighbors pretending to be the police. Tell them there's been a rash of backyard dog abductions. Advise them to keep their dogs inside for at least a year.

13) When the dogs finally stop barking and fall asleep around 4:30 a.m., tiptoe up to them and yell, "It's about freaking time!"

14) Go to the pet store and purchase a large bucket of "Bark-Be-Gone." Apply liberally.

15) Ignore them. They'll stop ... yeah, just like that bully in junior high.

16) Eat lots of vegetables, exercise, take your vitamins, and outlive the hairy beasts by sixty years.

17) They say that living well is the best revenge, so buy a ten-year-old Chevy, drink wine that has a screw cap instead of a cork, and take a vacation to Dollywood.

18) Enroll in that community college continuing education course about dog mind control that you've always wanted to take but couldn't quite fit into your schedule.

19) Walk by the windows naked every few minutes. That should confuse them into silence.

20) Go to the library and check out a book about dog behavior. Make sure it's a really big book. Throw it at them. Throw it hard.

21) Radio their coordinates to central command.

22) Read the dogs that notebook full of love poems you wrote in tenth grade.

23) Throw the dogs a surprise birthday party. Get a poodle in

a bikini to jump out of a cake.

24) Become friends with the neighborhood kid who's really good with his slingshot. Invite him over for target practice.

25) Take up the tuba. Practice late at night in the part of your yard closest to your neighbors' bedroom window.

26) Move. Now.

27) When your neighbor comes out on the porch at midnight and says, "Will my sweet puppies please stop their barkie-warkies? Who're my good boys? Yes, you are, yes, you're my good boys, yes, you are, oh, my pookie-wookie puppies!" videotape the whole thing. Make sure your lawyer gets the tape into evidence at your trial. No jury would convict you.

28) Take comfort in the fact that only *cats* have nine lives.

29) Enter your neighbors in one of those "win-a-year-long-vacation-to-Madagascar" contests at the local mall. Make sure it's the one that allows the winners to bring pets.

30) Join a support group. Confront your feelings. Get in touch with your inner child. Make peace with your demons. Don't be afraid to cry.

31) Contact that horse whisperer guy. Ask him if he does dogs.

32) Begin a novel with the line, "It was a dark and stormy night, and my neighbors' dogs were barking again." Begin looking for a literary agent to handle this can't-miss bestseller.

33) Write a complaint letter to former President Bush. If anyone can help with such a difficult diplomatic situation, it's "W."

34) Mark your territory. You know what this means, and so will the dogs.

35) Help the dogs open a dot.com business. That should make them disappear pretty quickly.

36) Knit each dog a really nice sweater—maybe some booties and scarves as well. They've probably just been trying to tell you that they're a little chilly.

37) Just bark right back at the smelly bastards and see how they like it.

Wrong Number

While in graduate school, Sally paid the bills for a year by working part-time at a weird little fast-food restaurant at the local mall. They specialized in french fries, so the place was called the "French Fry Factory." For uniforms, they wore bright yellow T-shirts and baseball caps emblazoned with the glowing orange words, "French Fry Factory." (Just for fun, the "o" in "factory" was shaped like a cog.) In the fluorescent mall lighting, that yellow and orange combination was almost enough to cook the fries by itself.

The place had a small dining area with six tables and an open food-prep area so that anybody walking by could stare at Sally while she worked. She was often alone, taking orders and operating the cash register with her right hand and reaching back to run the fryers and the grill with her left.

The job paid minimum wage, and Sally got one free sandwich and all the fries and drinks she wanted during each shift. All in all, it wasn't a bad deal. Each day, she skipped breakfast and lunch, then snacked on fries and iced tea while she worked. When her shift ended, she would settle down for a leisurely burger and do some reading for her night classes. She hardly ever bought groceries that year, even stopping in for free fries on her occasional days off, and she actually lost fifteen pounds because the work kept her too busy to eat much.

Within a couple of weeks, Sally got "promoted" to "opener." There was no extra pay, but she got to come in at 9 a.m. and open the place—a much better job than "closer" at 10 p.m. Mornings were quiet at the mall, and she was able to develop a routine that made the job easy. She enjoyed having a couple of calm hours of light duty before the lunch rush began.

When she'd been there for about three months, Sally's morning quiet was interrupted by a phone call at precisely

9:30.

"Hello, French Fry Factory!" she sang out in her cheeriest voice.

An elderly sounding woman on the other end of the line said, "I would like to speak to Marion, please."

"I'm sorry, ma'am," Sally replied. "There's no one here by that name. I think you might have the wrong number."

The woman recited the phone number and again asked for Marion.

"That's the right number," Sally said, "but this is the French Fry Factory. We're a restaurant in the mall, not a residence."

"Marion said I should call her at this number," the woman continued, sounding frustrated.

"I'm really sorry," Sally said, "but there's no Marion here."

The woman abruptly hung up. Sally shrugged and sent the woman a silent wish that she would find her Marion, and then got back to work.

The next morning, the phone rang again at 9:30.

"Hello, French Fry Factory!"

"I would like to speak with Marion, please." The same voice.

"I'm sorry, but this is the French Fry Factory again."

"Marion said she'd be there." This time, there seemed to be a hint of panic.

"I'm really sorry, ma'am. Do you have a last name for Marion? Maybe I could help you look up her number."

"She said she would be there," the woman snapped and hung up.

For months, these calls continued—not every day, sometimes not even every week, but always at 9:30. Each time, the woman seemed reluctant to believe that Marion wasn't waiting expectantly for her call. And each time, she hung up before Sally could say anything helpful.

This was back before caller-ID, so Sally investigated. She asked the other "openers" if they ever got any wrong-number calls. Most of them said they didn't, but one guy said he refused to answer the phone before 10:30 when they officially opened for business. He eventually admitted that he may have heard the phone ring a few times in the morning, but he stuck to his philosophy that if they weren't open, he shouldn't have to answer the phone.

As the months went along, Sally tried several strategies. She started answering the 9:30 calls by saying, "Hello?" in a pleasant voice, as if she were a retiree in the middle of morning coffee. That didn't help. Sometimes she picked up the phone and didn't say anything, but the woman would just hang up after a few seconds. Sally even answered a few times with, "Please don't hang up. I want to help you find Marion." But the woman would repeat, "Marion should be there," and then hang up. Once Sally even answered, "Hello, information ... could I please have the last name of the party you are trying to reach?" No luck—all she heard was a click.

Sally didn't remember exactly when the calls stopped, but one day she realized that the woman hadn't called in a month. In the meantime, Sally had finished her master's degree and was about to leave the French Fry Factory and move out of the area.

During Sally's last week, the manager held a surprise going-away party. Most of her co-workers were there, and several of the handsome guys who worked at the clothing stores in the mall (and whom Sally had often treated to free coffee) stopped by to kiss her cheek. The unexpected pleasure of this party nearly brought Sally to tears as she realized how much this silly little job had meant to her for the past year.

The owner even showed up. He was a lawyer who hardly ever came to the store. Sally heard that he operated the restaurant as a tax write-off and was upset when they actually started turning a profit. But he seemed like a nice enough guy, and Sally was glad he came to say good-bye.

With the owner was a very tiny woman. She had bright, happy eyes, and Sally could tell she had once been young and active. She still maintained an energy and a glow that made her very appealing.

"This is my grandmother, Mrs. Candelaria," the owner said after shaking Sally's hand and wishing her luck.

"Oh, Glen, don't be so formal," the woman scolded her grandson. Then she turned to Sally and smiled, extending her hand.

"Please, call me Marion."

Not Getting Flirted With at the Gym

Rob joined a gym recently, not to get in shape so much as to meet women. The wives of his friends have told him, in the presence of their husbands, that he's not an unattractive man in a not terribly unhandsome way. Four negatives equal a positive—that's how Rob is reading that assessment. Rob's friends' wives tell him the gym is a great place to meet women, so he has been going five or six times a week. Even so, he's not getting flirted with at the gym.

A recent Friday night trip to the gym was a pretty typical example of Rob's plight. When he arrived and slid his key card through the little slot that makes his photo appear on a computer screen at the front desk, the pretty woman working behind the desk smiled, said hi and wished Rob a happy workout. She was so professional and nice, but Rob was there to get flirted with, not visit with the cute receptionist, so he nodded to her and headed toward the exercise machines.

At the treadmill, a woman made eye-contact with Rob. "I'm so silly," she said. "I just can't seem to figure out how to program this machine. Can you help me, please?"

Rob was on a mission to get flirted with, but he took about ten seconds to program her treadmill for her. She smiled the whole time and acted very grateful when he finished. *Are these machines really that hard for her to figure out?* Rob thought. *It's just a couple of buttons.* He didn't want to waste time programming other people's exercise machines. Rob needed to focus his time on getting flirted with.

Rob brought a book to read on the exercise bike. He usually spent lots of time glancing sideways to see what other people are reading, so he figured women would probably be curious about his book, *Pigs in Heaven* by Barbara Kingsolver. He hoped that a book like this would show what a sensitive man he is. Combined with the hard-muscled body he was sure he would get from working out here, the women wouldn't be able to help but flirt with him.

After he'd been reading for about ten minutes, an attractive older woman took his literary bait. "Pigs in heaven?" she asked. "That sounds like a book about my first husband, except for the heaven part!" She laughed and lingered for a few seconds, but by this point, Rob was really absorbed in the book and wondered what would happen to sweet little Turtle and her accidental adoptive mother, so he hardly noticed when she shrugged and walked away.

Half an hour later, his bike beeped to tell him that he'd finished his programmed workout. *Gosh*, Rob thought, *the time and the pages just flew by*. The number of flirt-potential women around the exercise machines was pretty thin, so he headed downstairs to the weight room.

On the way there, he met an acquaintance of his ex-girlfriend. For the life of him, Rob couldn't remember her name. "Hi Rob!" she called out the second she saw him. She was carrying a racquetball racquet. Rob had played racquetball often, so they talked for a while about the sport. She had just started playing a few weeks before and hadn't been able to find a partner.

"Yeah," she said, a bit downcast, "I can't find anyone to play with me, so I've just been playing with myself every chance I get." Then she brightened. "Hey, would you like to play with me?"

"Oh, I'm sorry," Rob replied. "I've been playing for a long time, mostly with really athletic men, so playing with you wouldn't be much fun for either of us." She must have been in a rush to get to the court because she excused herself and hurried off.

The evening was rapidly getting away from Rob, and he hadn't been flirted with once the whole time, so he headed over to the weights. Right away, two women caught his eye. Both were in great shape with thick-muscled backs and arms. He pulled a couple of dumbbells from the rack next to the women and started working on biceps curls. As much as he tried for the next twenty minutes, he couldn't seem to get their attention. He followed them from station to station, but they were focused only on each other and the weights.

The more they ignored him, the more Rob was drawn to them. It was almost a turn-on to watch them spot each other with the weights, each one taking turns grasping the other's arms or legs or waist to help with the exercise. They must have been sisters or neighbors to be that close. *They probably have weight-lifter husbands at home,* Rob thought, *so there isn't much chance of them flirting with me.*

Rob was just about ready to leave because it was becoming pretty obvious to him that this gym wasn't much of a hotspot to get flirted with. But a strange thing happened that made him stay a bit longer. He was actually getting into his workout. For weeks, he'd been coming to the gym hoping to meet women without even a single bite on his line. The exercise machines and weights had been little more than props to give him something to do while waiting for women to flirt with him. But he started to notice that there might actually be something more to the gym than just sexual tension. So he sat down at the butterfly machine to work on his chest muscles for a few minutes before heading home.

"Oh, sorry," Rob heard a woman's voice say. He felt a little bump to his left as he hefted the machine's handle on that side. Those machines were really close together, and she must have accidentally brushed against that side of the machine as he pulled the weights along their path.

"That's okay," Rob replied as he completed the last four repetitions, feeling his chest expand with each lift.

As he rested after his set, he heard the same woman sneeze. It was a really cute, petite, little sneeze.

"Bless you," Rob said automatically.

"Thank you," she replied. "It's so nice to hear a man say that. Most men these days just ignore you when you sneeze."

Rob looked directly at her for the first time. She was about his age, maybe a little older, with a very pretty face. She was slender and in good shape, like she'd been coming to the gym often. She wore a pink top that worked well for her and black leggings. She was a real blonde, not dyed—Rob was an observant person who could tell about such things. And she was smiling at him. It dawned on him for the first time that night that he might actually be getting flirted with. Rob didn't quite know what to do. Should he wait to see what would happen? Or should he think up something witty to say and flirt back?

Whether she was flirting or not, Rob decided he wasn't interested anyway. He said a quick, "Well, goodnight," grabbed his sweatshirt and book, and headed toward the door. It was, after all, a Friday night. Did Rob really want to invest his time flirting with someone who couldn't get a date and had to spend Friday night at the gym?

Relation Translation

1) *Relation:* I've *never* been in a singles bar before.
Translation: I'm here *every* night, and I'm desperate to meet *anybody.*
2) *Relation:* Would you like another drink?
Translation: How many more drinks will it take to get you rip-snorting drunk?
3) *Relation:* What do you do for a living?
Translation: How much money do you have in the bank right now, and how much of that can I sponge from you before you wise up?
4) *Relation:* What do you usually do with your free time?
Translation: Are you as lonely and miserable as you seem to be?
5) *Relation:* I've admired you from a distance for a long time.
Translation: When your back is turned, I stare at your rear end every chance I get.
6) *Relation:* I know we've just met, but I feel like I've known you for a long time.
Translation: Please go to bed with me!
7) *Relation:* I love you.
Translation: I love *me.*
8) *Relation:* You can trust me.
Translation: Look what a great liar I am.
9) *Relation:* I've never met anyone quite like you before.
Translation: In six months, I can have you trained to act just like my ex-lover, who is a *much* better person than you.
10) *Relation:* It's been a long time since I've met someone as special as you.
Translation: I've been going out with some seriously dull people lately.
11) *Relation:* I feel so lucky to be with you tonight.
Translation: I feel so lucky that one of my tired pick-up lines finally worked.

12) *Relation:* I love you.
Translation: You love me.
13) *Relation:* I'm divorced.
Translation: If you marry me, I will divorce you and make you suffer like no one has ever suffered before.
14) *Relation:* I like to work out and stay in shape.
Translation: I like my body much better than yours.
15) *Relation:* What sports do you like?
Translation: I'd like to see your rear end in spandex.
16) *Relation:* I love you.
Translation: I am weak and needy.
17) *Relation:* I don't watch much television.
Translation: I'm testing you to prove that I'm intellectually superior to you.
18) *Relation:* Mine is the BMW.
Translation: I have so much money that you should be *thrilled* to sleep with me.
19) *Relation:* My last lover was kind of inhibited.
Translation: I'm a raving sex pervert.
20) *Relation:* Would you like to go out for dinner and a movie tonight?
Translation: Would you like to have brief, superficial sex very late tonight, and then have me get dressed as fast as I can, rush home, and not call you for six weeks?
21) *Relation:* Your past doesn't bother me.
Translation: It's obvious that you used to be an amoral user, but I'm so wonderful that my presence alone will change you into a totally giving human being.
22) *Relation:* You have a beautiful smile.
Translation: Why are you always in such a bad mood?
23) *Relation:* I think you're very intelligent.
Translation: You're smart enough to agree with me as often as possible.
24) *Relation:* I love you.
Translation: You are weak and needy.

25) *Relation:* What restaurants around here have a good salad bar?

Translation: You're fat.

26) *Relation:* Let's just spend a quiet evening alone together.

Translation: I'm extremely bored with your friends and the places you like to go and the things you like to do.

27) *Relation:* Let's go out with some friends tonight.

Translation: The thought of spending the evening alone with you terrorizes me with boredom.

28) *Relation:* I'll pick you up at seven o'clock.

Translation: I'll probably pick you up by eight o'clock if I haven't met anyone I like better than you by then.

29) *Relation:* I'd love to take you for a long walk deep in the woods where we can be alone together in the beauty of nature.

Translation: I'm ashamed to be seen in public with you.

30) *Relation:* Oh my god, you're so wonderful!

Translation: You're almost as good as my last lover, but you still need a lot of work.

31) *Relation:* Did you change your hairstyle, honey?

Translation: Why the hell did you let someone mutilate you like that, you idiot?

32) *Relation:* What do you think of my new haircut, honey?

Translation: Right this minute, give me 247 compliments, each one more lavish than the one before.

33) *Relation:* You're the best lover I've ever had.

Translation: You'll believe *anything* I tell you.

34) *Relation:* I'm sorry, but I have to work this weekend.

Translation: I'd rather spend the weekend doing *anything other than seeing you.*

35) *Relation:* I really care about you, but my career is very important to me.

Translation: The work I do to make enough money to buy toilet paper is more important to me than you are.

36) *Relation:* I promise I'll never leave you.

Translation: I'm about to be arrested for insider trading.

37) *Relation:* Can I help you with that?

Translation: I'm so much smarter and more talented than you, so I'd better do that or else you'll screw it up beyond repair.

38) *Relation:* I think you're a great cook, but I'd like to take you out for a nice dinner tonight.

Translation: You can't even fry Spam without an instruction booklet.

39) *Relation:* You're an extremely nice person.

Translation: You certainly are a boring blob of nothingness, aren't you?

40) *Relation:* I'm extremely fond of you.

Translation: Try to have a serious relationship with me, and I'll be on the next plane to Portugal.

41) *Relation:* You're the best friend I've ever had.

Translation: I wouldn't sleep with you again if you begged me.

42) *Relation:* I'm afraid things just aren't working out between us.

Translation: I'm dumping you now, and I'm going to degrade you with tons of pity while I'm doing it.

43) *Relation:* It's nobody's fault.

Translation: It's *your* fault.

44) *Relation:* I'm really sorry that I hurt your feelings.

Translation: You now have my permission to stop complaining and acting like such a baby.

45) *Relation:* I love you.

Translation: I *own* you.

46) *Relation:* Of course I'm listening to you.

Translation: If I don't tell you that I'm listening to you, you'll get furious, but the truth is that everything you say is so incredibly dull that I can feel the life-blood slipping out of me with every word you speak.

47) *Relation:* I'm not sure that I understand what you're trying to say.

Translation: You're ranting again.

48) *Relation:* I'm not sure that you understand what I'm trying to say.
Translation: You're stupid.
49) *Relation:* How about if you wait for me to call you?
Translation: My lawyer is filing the restraining order tomorrow.
50) *Relation:* I don't know whether or not any one human being can fully satisfy all the needs of any other human being.
Translation: I'm already dating someone else.

One Bite

Back in his college days, partly on a dare, partly from fatigue, and partly for love, Tony ate an entire jelly-filled donut in one bite.

Tony and three friends had gone to an all-night donut shop to blow off steam during final exams week. For college students, they weren't terribly rebellious considering there were about a dozen bars in the area. But who needs alcohol when there are donuts to be consumed?

They were the only customers in the place at 2:30 a.m., munching on at least their fourth donut each. The combination of study fatigue, suddenly full stomachs, and post-sugar buzz had set in hard, so they were in danger of falling asleep right there at the table. Something had to be done to liven them up before they drove back to the dorm to continue studying.

So Tony slammed both palms on the stained table top and announced, "I can eat an entire jelly-filled donut in one bite!"

His friends jumped about six inches out of their seats and started shouting protests.

"No one can do that!" Sarah cried.

"I say bull crap on your donut!" Mike ranted. Mike was pre-med. He had taken a biology final the previous day and a chemistry final that morning, and he was dreading a physics final the following afternoon. His head was overstuffed with science, and he moved between anger and frustration, shouts and tears, more than a few times that week.

"If you can do it," Susan said with a smile, "I just might marry you."

"Why?" Sarah asked.

"Think about it," Susan replied.

"Oh," Sarah said.

Mike tried for a few seconds, but his brain couldn't work out what they meant. Tony himself had only a slight inkling, but an inkling that certainly made him look at Susan in a new way.

Sarah smiled at Tony and pushed a blueberry-filled pastry toward him. Blueberry was his favorite. It was the last one left on the table.

"I've been saving this one," she said. "If you can eat it in one bite, I won't marry you, but I'll give you a dollar."

"Me too!" Mike and Susan chimed. Three dollars—this was getting interesting. Tony was a poor college student who saw actual paper money about twice a month. Three whole dollars qualified as an academic scholarship.

The donut was about four inches in diameter and two inches thick. Powdered sugar covered the surface, and blueberry jelly oozed from a dime-sized navel on one side. The thing looked pretty darned big as Tony examined it. Under normal circumstances, he would have needed maybe seven or eight good bites to get it down. But then he'd probably think, *Wow, that was so small. How about another?*

He picked it up. It seemed to weigh a pound because, Tony assumed, jelly is heavy stuff. Three pairs of measuring eyes darted back and forth from his mouth to the donut. Tony turned the navel toward him to prevent spillage and brought it to his lips.

On the first push, a third of the donut easily entered his mouth, but then he encountered resistance. Tony had to shove first the left side and then the right side to keep it advancing beyond the corners of his mouth.

This trundle method worked fine until the donut encountered his uvula, the little flap of flesh at the back of the throat. Tony started to gag. He mustered all his self-control to keep from yanking the thing out of his mouth. At this point, the first tear plopped out of his eye and trickled down his cheek.

Tony kept pushing.

The donut crammed up against the back of his throat and started expanding upward into his pallet and downward under his tongue. By then, it had lost most of its structural integrity, becoming nothing more than a fused blob of pastry and jelly conforming to the inside of his mouth.

Tears began to flow freely now, and some sort of liquid threatened to spill from his nose as well. Tony sniffed as forcefully as he could, snorting up a big dose of powdered sugar in the process. Every force in his body urged him to expel this thing from his mouth.

But Tony kept pushing.

A few more corner tucks, and the donut was inside. He clasped his teeth together and sealed his lips.

"Jeebus," Mike gasped.

"He did it," Sarah said.

"Not yet," Susan cut in. "I won't marry him unless he swallows.

The three of them began chanting, *"Swallow, swallow, swallow."* They started with a whisper, then built to a low moan. *"Swallow, swallow, swallow."*

For human beings, chewing usually precedes swallowing. So Tony parted his teeth and closed them again, then repeated the movement a few times, being careful not to open his lips—not out of politeness, but to keep donut paste from spraying across the room.

Normally, the tongue is used to roll the food around the mouth so that it gets ground up by the teeth. But this process takes lots of open space, something Tony had none of in his mouth, filled as it was with donut. His chewing efforts managed only to mush up the small fraction of pastry directly between his molars.

In short, the whole mess was stuck in Tony's mouth with no real way for him to chew it. In fact, it was actually expanding as it soaked up his saliva at an alarming rate. To keep his cheeks from bursting open, he had to do something fast.

"Swallow, swallow, swallow," they chanted.

Tony's gag reflex came to his rescue. As he involuntarily

tightened the back of his throat, he could feel those muscles smashing a small portion of the donut back there. In desperation, he clamped down harder and found he could actually "chew" with his throat muscles.

After a few more contractions, the donut was soft enough to get some down. Tony swallowed a small portion, freeing up enough mouth space to guide more donut to the back of his throat where he muscle-chewed and got a bit more down.

"Swallow, swallow, swallow."

Tony then discovered that he had freed up just enough room to do a little traditional teeth chewing. This was tough going, but it began to work. Bit by bit, he managed to swallow more and more of the donut until the task didn't seem quite so impossible.

"Oh my God," Sarah muttered, breaking the chant. "I think he's going to do it."

It took another full minute, but Tony was able to get the rest of the thing swallowed. His throat burned. His face was streaked with tears. Sometime during the process, he had lost control of his nose. The results were not pretty.

Susan grabbed a handful of napkins and mopped Tony's face. "That was amazing!" she said, leaning in to kiss him on the cheek. When she pulled away, Tony saw tiny flecks of powdered sugar on her lips. He'd never really looked at Susan's lips before, but he was having trouble looking anywhere else at that moment. Her tongue slipped out to lick the sugar from her lower lip, the fuller of the two.

"I don't believe it," Mike said. "Make him open his mouth."

Susan gently grasped Tony's jaw and opened his mouth to display its lack of donut.

"Ugh," Sarah moaned. Apparently, there was still some donut residue in there. Tony took a swig of hot chocolate (now cold), rinsed it around his mouth, swallowed, and opened again.

"I'll be goose downed," Mike gasped.

"He did it!" Sarah cried.

The three of them broke into applause, nearly awakening the high school kid snoozing through his late-night shift behind the counter.

Susan gathered up the three one-dollar bills from the table and tucked them into her shirt pocket.

"I'll just hold onto these," she said. "My abnormal psych final is over at noon tomorrow. If you meet me at the student union, I'll buy you an ice cream cone." She winked at Tony. "I'm dying to see what you can do with that."

Six Questions

January 7, 1973

"Am I going to have to pull this car over?"

The shiver Jack felt came half from the winter air rushing in through the car's gaping rear window and half from the tone he recognized in his mother's gravelly voice. Jack's older sister beside him in the back seat huddled deeper into her winter coat and stared at the front seat headrests a foot from her face, familiar with this repeated drama since Jack had learned to talk a decade ago.

"I'd rather freeze than choke," Jack said.

"Bob, please talk to him," Sandi, Jack's mother, implored.

Jack's father turned from the driver's seat to look at his son. Bob's cigarette clung to his lower lip with dried spit, dangling and disregarding gravity.

"Can't you just ignore it, Jack? It's just a little smoke," Bob said, turning his gaze back to the highway as tiny bits of ash fell onto the shoulder of his thick canvas jacket. He brushed the ashes away, leaving a thin charcoal streak.

Everyone hunched into themselves for a few seconds before Jack's mother broke the silence.

"I can't even enjoy a simple cigarette without him making a big production out of things," Sandi said, crushing her cigarette out in the ashtray. Bob cracked the window and tossed his out.

"Are you happy now?" Jack's sister asked through chattering teeth.

"Not really," Jack answered as he rolled up his window.

September 22, 1979

"Why not her?"

Gary pointed to a slender brunette three tables away in the crowded cafeteria. Even three tables away, Jack knew which girl Gary meant.

Her name was Heather. Jack only knew that because a guy named Jerry in biology class told Jack her name and said that he overheard Heather saying she thought Jack was "cute." Jerry and Heather went to the same high school.

Jack had only been in college for two weeks, and he hadn't met any girls yet. He hadn't really been trying. After going to a tiny high school where he had been labeled "homely" since first grade, it was hard to get used to being at a college where girls might think he was "cute."

Heather and some of her friends got up to leave. Jack liked the way they looked in their sorority sweatpants, a Greek letter stitched onto each half of their rear ends. Jack liked watching the Greek letters move when Heather walked toward the doors. But he didn't like the way she reached for the bulge in the side pocket of her sweatpants when she and her friends reached the cafeteria door. He didn't like the way she drew a wrinkled, shiny package to her mouth

"Why not?" Gary asked again.

"She's a junior," Jack replied. "She wouldn't be interested in me."

June 18, 1989

"Is this your grandson?"

The nurse massaged her fingertips into the blooming bruises at the crook of Jack's mother's arm. "I'm sure we can find another vein here somewhere," she said.

Jack leaned forward and kissed his mother's cheek. She smiled and readjusted the silk scarf he had given her yesterday to cover her bald head. She didn't like the wig that the hospital had supplied.

"My son," Jack's mother croaked. "My youngest. My baby."

"Oh," said the nurse.

Jack's mother glanced up at the television suspended from the wall near the ceiling. The sound was turned off. A game show was in progress, and someone had just lost a large sum of money that was never really his anyway.

"Here we go," the nurse said, sliding the new IV needle into Jack's mother's arm.

February 14, 2000

"Smoking or non-smoking?"

The waitress looked familiar, but Jack couldn't tell where he had seen her. She was smiling at him and completely ignoring Amy. Their third date happened to fall on Valentine's Day. The sitter was with Amy's daughter Linda at home, so Jack and Amy had the whole evening ahead of them.

Before Jack could speak, Amy waved the rose Jack had given her earlier in the evening through the waitress's line of vision, making her blink and turned her gaze toward Amy.

"Smoking," Amy said.

June 4, 2003

"Does my mom smoke?"

Linda's ten-year-old confidence usually carried her voice, so Jack was surprised at how small she sounded in the front seat of his car. In the three years he had been dating Amy, Linda's mother, the girl had never seemed so young and small. It was just the two of them, gliding along through the nighttime rain on the way home from her violin lesson. The wipers ticked three times before Jack could respond.

"What makes you ask that?" He glanced over and saw Linda looking directly at him. Even in the poor light, he could see the intensity in her gaze that he couldn't hear in her voice.

"Well," she said, not taking her eyes from his face, "I've been wondering for a long time. I keep finding used-up cigarettes in the toilet and the trash can. I'm not looking for them or anything, but they're hard to miss. And sometimes her bedroom smells like ashes."

Involuntarily, Jack took a sniff. Amy had borrowed his car last week while he took hers in to have the brakes serviced. Jack glanced at the ashtray and wondered what surprises it contained.

"Plus, my dad says she does lots of bad things," Linda continued. "But I'm never sure if I should believe what he says."

June 8, 2003

"What did you tell her?"

Amy leaned forward from her hiding place behind Jack and peered over his shoulder toward the lake. Linda splashed with two of her friends in the shallows just beyond the edge of the beach. Suddenly the three of them sprinted out into the water until it reached their thighs. They dove and began swimming toward the dock with the diving board near the center of the lake. Linda was the best swimmer of the three.

Amy relaxed behind Jack and took a long draw on her cigarette, now that Linda could not possibly see her. Jack could hear the hot crackling and feel the ember's heat near his bare shoulder as she inhaled. He leaned forward.

"I told her how much it bothered me that my parents smoked when I was a kid," Jack said to Amy, not turning to look at her. "I told her that sometimes people have a very hard time quitting, even when they really want to.

Amy ground her cigarette into the beach and covered the butt with a few handfuls of sand.

"You could have just told her that I don't smoke," Amy said.

Linda was already on the diving board when her slower-swimming friends reached the dock and scampered up the ladder to join her.

"That wouldn't be true," Jack said.

Linda ran down the diving board and let out a long squeal as she flung herself into a cannonball that showered her friends with lake water.

"I wish you had told her …" Amy started but didn't finish her thought. "I wish I didn't …" she began again, and then she rose from the blanket and walked toward the car.

Character Sketch

Aaron has been staring at this thing for an hour now, barely able to move, his rear end stuck in his desk chair exactly where it landed when he went weak in the knees at the first glance. He knows what this means. He knows who they are and how all of this must have happened. He has an appointment with them—and his destiny—at two o'clock this afternoon. He reconstructed nearly every detail over the past hour, his mind unable to tear itself away from the implications. He has spent his whole life wondering about all of this—but now he knows. His only problem is that he has no idea in the world what to do next.

* * *

It all started yesterday. Aaron was at the mall, as usual, the same booth where he camped out five hours each day, five days a week, for almost a decade now. Aaron sketches children in his booth—but not the way you might think. This is a unique gig he has going for himself, absolutely one of a kind. Sure, lots of people do this with photographs, but that's easy. He poked around the Internet a few years ago to see if he had any drawing competition, but he found himself to still be the first, last, and only that he could find.

You see, Aaron doesn't draw *real live children* dragged to the mall by shopping parents. None of that for him. Too much squirming and complaining and screaming when someone tries to sketch the kids themselves. Too much depressing family crap for his taste—parents either way too proud or way too critical, inflicting lifelong harm on the poor little schmucks with nearly every word.

Instead, Aaron draws *potential* children. Here's how it works: A couple will sit at his booth, and he'll make sketches of them, which takes about fifteen minutes for both people.

He knows he's no great artist, but he has a good eye for faces and an easy, fluent line with the pencil. So, once he's done with their portraits, he tells them that he's going to take the sketches home, meditate on them, and then draw pictures of four kids that they could have if they decided they wanted to give parenthood a whirl. The next time they come in, they can pay him a pitiful five bucks for the original portraits of themselves or fifty bucks for five renderings of their potential kids.

You know what? Aaron gets the fifty bucks every time.

It seems nobody can resist drawings of their potential kids. About half the time, he gets folks who really don't have kids and want to know what their offspring might look like. But he also gets the other half: folks who have kids already and want to see how close his drawings come to the real tykes—kind of like guess-my-weight at the county fair. And his customers are always satisfied. The no-kids-yet people take one look and swoon, probably ready to go home and take a crack at procreation that very day just because they fell in love with one or all of their potential kid drawings. The guess-my-weights, most of whom figured him as a fraud and just want to show him up, are dumbfounded. At least one, usually two or three of his drawings are dead ringers for their progeny. Even if they didn't bring the cash with them, one look at his pictures sends them sprinting for a bank machine.

So how does he do it? Is this a mystical gift bestowed upon him in a meditative trance? Well, that's what Aaron wants the customers to believe, but only because it gets them to recommend him to their friends. The truth is he's actually *half* fraud. He takes his parent sketches home and scans them into his computer, and then runs a program he designed to generate a dozen possible kid combinations. He calls the program "Gregor," after the monk that did all those genetics experiments Aaron red about in the orphanage library as a kid. Someday he'll sell the program and make a fortune, but he's not ready to retire his act just yet. It only takes about an hour to run a full day's sketches, usually ten or fifteen couples. Then he takes the output—these strange, shaded, little computer-generated snapshots—picks the most interesting four, and does quick-and-dirty sketches of each one.

All in all, it's five hours of drawing and schmoozing and handing out pictures to amazed customers at the mall, an hour feeding the computer each night, and another two hours in the morning to do the kid sketches—an eight-hour day, just like any other hard-working American, except Aaron is his own boss. He takes lots of days off, and he clears about seventy grand a year. Not bad for an orphan from the wrong side of Charleston, West Virginia's tracks.

His present predicament began yesterday afternoon. He was finishing up sketches of a mid-thirties couple, real yuppie types straight from the dressing rooms at Banana Republican, all denim and chinos, light blues and washed tans. These were guess my-weights, he figured, even though they didn't admit it. They probably had three carpet-climbers imprisoned in the minivan twenty rows back in the parking lot, gasping for air in the three o'clock heat.

"We're just so interested in what our kids *might* look like," Mr. Dad said, proud parenthood dripping from the corner of his mouth. A dead giveaway, his emphasis on "might."

"Oh, I wonder what you'll come up with," Mrs. Mom said, looking at Aaron wide-eyed as if to say either, "My kids are much more beautiful than anything you could ever draw" or "They're monsters from the deep, here to make my life a living hell." It's pretty strange how similar wonderful parents and possible infanticiders really are.

While Aaron was busy sketching their attractive yet vacant faces, he noticed an older couple hanging around, moving casually, trying not to be noticed, and, in doing so, sticking out like a three-armed fish. They hovered near the neighboring stores, eyes seeming to stare intently at rows of greeting cards and racks of personalized pencils, occasionally shooting a corner-of-the-eye glance in Aaron's direction.

When they weren't sneaking looks at him, he would sneak looks at them, glancing away from his yuppie customers while he pretended to root around for another pencil or to get a different perspective on his emerging sketch. They looked about sixty or so, weekenders, he in jeans and madras shirt, she in a white T-shirt under summer dress, both with that healthy gleam you see in older folks a lot these days, all active minds and fiberful digestions.

The woman was very tall, probably six feet in flat sandals, nearly as tall as Aaron was himself, a couple of inches taller than the man, and not a bit stooped by age. Despite his powers of spying, Aaron couldn't get much of a fix on her face, except to see that it was broad and full featured beneath a thick froth of wavy, gray hair. The man was wide across the shoulders, the madras plaid making him look like a senior-division body builder, knotty arms twisting from his sleeves. His hair was half-black, half-white, almost striped in a way that could only be natural.

As Aaron finished up with Mr. Dad and Mrs. Mom, he ignored their smug winks to each other. They promised to meet him there tomorrow afternoon. Aaron already started dreading the seconds as they skipped away. He put their sketches with the others he'd done that day, and then turned around to see that the older couple had marched right up to him—no more sneaking around.

"Hi there," the woman said. That was a switch because people usually start out with something witty like, "Hey, are you doing drawings?"

"Hello," Aaron replied, polite to a fault, partly because he had to deal well with the public to make a living and partly because these people just seemed too nice for anything but honest courtesy.

"We like your portraits," the man said, admiring the finished drawings of the couple that just left. That was unusual as well. People didn't usually compliment his work until they saw the magic children sketches.

"Thank you," Aaron replied.

He started to explain his gig, but the woman cut him off.

"Oh, we know," she said. "We've been watching you today. And we've heard a lot of good things about your work."

Now that was different. No one ever called what Aaron did, "his work." Mostly people thought he was kind of a hack even when they like the results. Aaron's artist friends looked down on him as some kind of sellout for getting paid to draw, and his other friends thought he had the easiest job in the world.

"We'd like you to draw us," the man said.

"And make those pictures of our children," the woman said.

"Are we too old?" the man asked.

Aaron laughed. "I always say that you're never too old to have your picture drawn. Anything else is up to you."

He got the couple seated and took out his equipment—a big pad, an eraser, and a few pencils. The couple just sat there and looked at Aaron without speaking. At first, it was kind of strange but not really uncomfortable—at least not for Aaron. He focused on drawing, just as he always did. The pencil almost seemed to move on its own as he studied their faces, then studied the drawings, then their faces again.

The sketches took shape pretty quickly. The couple seemed to want to say something, but they were having trouble starting.

"So," Aaron said, getting the conversation rolling. "Do you live around here?"

"I'm originally from the Southeast," the woman said, and then she and her husband exchanged a look. "But we live in Kansas now," she added.

"We're here visiting relatives," the man said.

"Really?" Aaron replied, smudging a few pencil lines with his thumb to get the shadow under her cheekbone just right. "What relatives?"

"Our son," the woman said.

"Ah," Aaron replied, "so you have children. Are you getting these drawings done to compare them with your real kids?"

"Is that okay?" the woman asked.

"Sure," Aaron answered. "Lots of people do that." But they didn't usually tell him that's what they were doing. "How many children do you have?" he asked.

"Just our son," the man replied. "Do you have any children?"

This was a lot more personal than most people got. But something about these folks, some familiarity he couldn't quite define, made the question seem not so much like prying as honest interest.

"No," Aaron replied. "No kids. No wife. No girlfriend. It's just me. I was keeping a friend's dog for a while, but they guy decided not to come back from California, so I had to give him up for adoption."

"Oh my," the woman said, looking genuinely concerned.

"He went to a good home," Aaron said, focusing on finishing up the sketches while he rambled on a bit more than usual. "I actually wanted to keep him, but I'm not home enough during the day, and he got bored with me gone. He's with a family now, a friend of mine who has three kids and two other dogs. I visit sometimes, and they're all really happy together."

Aaron looked up from the drawing to find they were staring at him.

"I'm glad," the man said after a moment. And there was something in his look that made Aaron think he really meant it. Was this guy really just thinking about the dog? Aaron had a definite feeling that he had missed something in the conversation.

He stared at the point of his pencil for a full five seconds, a very long time in that situation actually, but he could find no answers in the rounded gray lead, so he put it away and got out a new sharp-tipped pencil. He stared at that one for five seconds as well, but it had nothing important to tell him either, so he told the couple that their drawings were done. Then they all stared at each other for another five seconds. Aaron hadn't done that much staring since his first crush on an orphanage nurse when he was seven.

"Well," Aaron said.

"Well," the man and woman both said.

"The drawings will be done tomorrow," Aaron said.

"We'll be here at two," the woman said.

"Is two okay?" the man asked. "You'll definitely be here?"

"I wouldn't miss it," Aaron said, and then wondered why he had put it exactly that way.

The couple smiled and shook Aaron's hand. They had walked fifty yards down the mall, glancing back three or four times, before Aaron realized that the people he draws hardly ever shake hands with him. Maybe it's the pencil lead stains, or maybe most people just don't care. Then he realized that he had forgotten to ask their names.

* * *

In the evening, Aaron went home and fed his sketches to the computer as usual. He barely glanced at most of them, basically different variations of the denim-and-chino couple, nothing extraordinary. But he looked for a long time at the older couple. The sketches were no better or worse than most of the ones he'd been doing for years. But in the pencil lines that made up these two faces were two attributes he wasn't accustomed to seeing in his own work: character and familiarity. The people in his sketches looked, as had the people in the flesh that day, like they were *somebody*, and, not only that, *somebody Aaron should know*.

Eventually, he roused himself from his blank-minded, mildly confused, fugue-state and scanned their drawings, typing in the shorthand commands that set the magical procreation program in motion. Sometimes that's how Aaron thought of it—as microchips procreating inside his computer. He slept well enough that night, stirring only once from a common-enough late-night thirst and an uncommon nagging sense that he had just emerged from a dream that he couldn't remember and didn't know whether or not he wanted to finish.

Aaron's morning routine was routine: rising early—a slow, half-hour jog with a ten-minute walk to cool down—a quick shave while the shower ran hot, steaming the mirror. All the while, he continued to wonder about the dream, but then he realized it wasn't the dream that had his mind turning unfamiliar corners. It was today's computer children. He seldom gave them a second thought before pulling them from the printer, taking a quick glance, and starting his morning sketches. But this morning, he practically ran from the bathroom to the printer, unsure why he needed to hurry. He tossed aside the yuppie kids and quickly found the dozen sheets that held the computer's mating of the older couple he had spent a strange half hour with yesterday.

The first eleven pictures were puzzles, just like the couple themselves—familiar strangers, enigmatic oxymoron's who stared at Aaron as if he were an amnesiac who had only recently forgotten who they were.

Then he got to the twelfth.

Aaron sat down hard and stayed there, gripping this one sheet for an hour so tensely that the paper tore a bit under his thumb. The likeness was amazing, truer than he would have thought possible. He'd seen the pictures taken of this face at the orphanage, ages two through sixteen, the last year, the year the foster parents came. In fact, he had those pictures in a box at the back of his closet, unseen for a decade or more, but clear as Kodak in the black and white of his memory.

At two o'clock that afternoon, Aaron would be meeting the parents of this face that won't release his stare, the same nice couple he met yesterday. He didn't know if he would keep that appointment. How could he? But how could he not?

The face stared up at him, young and innocent, but just a bit tired around the eyes, a trait those eyes still show, more appropriate now in adulthood. The curve of the jawline, the slight downward curl of the lips, the too-straight-line nose, the high forehead—those sad eyes—all there, all true.

The face on the sheet of paper, the face that stared back at Aaron with a thousand unasked questions, was his own.

About the Author

John Sheirer lives in Northampton, Massachusetts, with his wonderful wife Betsy. Also in attendance are his full-grown, terrific stepkids, Danielle and Daryl, and the happy memories of Daisy, the best dog in the world. He teaches at Asnuntuck Community College in Enfield, Connecticut, where he has been honored multiple times by *Who's Who Among America's Teachers*. He is a Pushcart Prize nominee, and his most recent books are the memoirs *Loop Year: 365 Days on the Trail*, winner of the Connecticut Green Circle Award, and *Growing Up Mostly Normal in the Middle of Nowhere,* a finalist for the Sante Fe Writers Project Literary Award. He is currently at work on a creative writing guidebook, *What's the Story? Fifty Photos to Kick-Start Your Writing* and can sometimes be found lurking here: www.johnsheirer.com.

www.ingramcontent.com/pod-product-compliance
Lightning Source LLC
Chambersburg PA
CBHW052134170626
46812CB00004B/1407